"What if we don't want to take orders from you?" the big man asked.

Kale looked at him, then suddenly conjured up a gun and shot him. The bullet smacked into his skull, whipping his head back viciously and jerking him part way around. Then, like a great tree, he slowly toppled over, smashing face down in the dirt of the yard, where he lay unmoving.

"Kilt him deader than a damned nit," the weasle-faced man observed, then looked up at Kale and said, "I reckon you made your point, Magician."

"Hell, then let's get back to our drinking," another man voted.

Nodding at the three dead men, Kale said, "Four of you fellers carry those things over to the south end of town and plant them. Reckon it's as good a time as any to start a boot hill."

Also in the LEATHERHAND series from Pinnacle Books

#6 THE MAGICIAN
MIKE WALES

PINNACLE BOOKS   NEW YORK

This novel is a work of fiction. Names, characters, places, and incidents are either the product of the author's imagination or are used fictitiously. Any resemblance to actual events or places or persons, living or dead, is entirely coincidental.

LEATHERHAND #6: THE MAGICIAN

Copyright © 1985 by Mike Wales

An original Pinnacle Books edition, published for the first time anywhere.

First printing/January 1985

ISBN: 0-523-42317-9

Can. ISBN: 0-523-43325-5

Printed in the United States of America .

PINNACLE BOOKS, INC.
1430 Broadway
New York, New York 10018

9 8 7 6 5 4 3 2 1

THE
MAGICIAN

Chapter I

The stage was on time. It was moving at a walk as Candy Hays, the driver, allowed his six-up to rest after the long hard run from Oracle to this spot on the San Pedro River. A half mile down the dusty track a sprawling adobe building sat beneath the limbs of an ironwood tree and two men busily harnessed and led out a change of horses, for they had heard Hays shouting curses at his teams and knew he would round the bend at any moment.

As Hays lined the stage out on the last lap to the Riverside Station, he glanced east toward the rimrocks and it was then he saw the tall man riding the Appaloosa. He sat the magnificent animal on a low hill 200 yards up a gentle slope, one leg hooked around the saddle horn, his hat slanted down to shade his face.

The stage rounded the bend, slammed down into the shallow waters of the San Pedro and lunged up the opposite bank as Hays put the horses under the whip, rolled into the station and came to a sliding, dust-tossing stop. The stage rocked on its thoroughbraces as Hays clambered down and shouted, "Riverside. Half hour for food, then we roll. Anyone not in the stage will be left behind," and stepped to the door, opened it and assisted a slim, well-dressed woman of about twenty-five to the ground.

1

She smiled at him and it smoothed the tired lines from her face and brought a quick flash of friendliness to her gray eyes.

"Thank you, Mr. Hays," she said and entered the station.

Following her from the stage was a tall officer wearing a 7th Cavalry patch on his tunic and the insignia of a colonel. Glancing around as if examining his surroundings with defense in mind, he too entered the station.

The third one out was a whiskey drummer, who had said he also sold guns and ladies' foundation garments. He was rotund, round-faced and his dark suit clung to him in ungainly folds, each wrinkle carrying a load of road dust. His bowler hat sat on the back of his head and, as he stepped clear of the stage, he tucked a cigar in the corner of his mouth and fired it up and the light from the match revealed cold, calculating eyes. Pushing back his coattails, he exposed a pair of perfectly matched Colt .45s in cutaway holsters. To Hays he was an enigma, for peddlers who came west were not given to toting guns. He entered the station.

A small, quiet-faced Chinese, whose age could have been anywhere from forty to sixty, stepped lightly to the ground, bowed slightly to Hays, who grinned and said, "Rough ride, Mr. Ah Kee?"

"It could have been smoother, but the road seems better than last year," Ah Kee answered in perfect English.

It was obvious Hays liked this quiet, dignified Chinese who owned half a dozen saloons in as many towns in southern Arizona and was reputed to be worth over a million dollars, although no one really knew for sure.

A disheveled young man, whose eyes were still filled with sleep, for that's what he had been doing for the last ten miles, stepped from the stage, tripped and, if Hays hadn't caught him, would have fallen flat.

"Keerful there, Wolf. You'll break your neck," Hays said.

The man called Wolf was in his early twenties, wore a pair of patched Levis, a gray shirt that had seen better days and a wide-brimmed black hat with a rattlesnake band around the crown. His outfit could have been replaced for two dollars, but not the guns he wore. They were well-oiled .44s equipped with stag horn handles. The filed away trigger guards and removed triggers marked him as a slip-hammer man, Hays knew, and from what the stage driver had heard, Wolf was deadly with those guns. Hays himself preferred to cock and then trigger his weapon, but Wolf's method was a faster one, once it had been mastered. All he had to do was draw, ear back the hammer and allow it to slip from beneath his thumb, then repeat the action. It eliminated the necessity of cocking and triggering the gun.

Slapping his hat against his leg, Wolf grinned and said, "I reckon I had me just a little too much of that tanglefoot over to Oracle. Makes a feller just a bit unsteady on his feet."

"Fun while it lasts," Hays observed. He had been known to take a drink.

The last man off the stage was that frontier breed, the professional gambler. This one had the cold, hard face and expressionless eyes of his calling, dressed all in black and carrying twin .45s, a very important part of his ensemble, for seldom did a week go by in his profession when some disgruntled player didn't decide to retrieve his money over a gambler's body.

He made Hays nervous. The stage driver had heard a lot of stories about this odd man, whose given name was Delta Kale, but who was known widely as the Magician because of his uncanny ability to manipulate cards. He also did occasional magic shows in which he made cards vanish, coins appears, watches stop ticking and wallets make unseen trips from one man's pocket to another's.

But it was his ability with guns that caused those who knew him to hold him in awe. He conjured them into his hands as if they were part of his magic act, and he never seemed to miss what he shot at.

Ducking his head, he entered the station and went directly to the crude bar, where he nodded at Bull Burke, the station manager, and asked for whiskey.

Removing a glass from the back bar, Burke ran a cloth around the inside of it, set it on the bar in front of the gambler and reaching beneath the plank, came up with a bottle. Pouring the glass full, Burke observed, "This here's the best whiskey you ever wrapped a lip around."

"Who makes it?" Kale asked, taking a sip.

"Injun over east of here in Dead Dog Canyon. Don't know where he learned the art, but by God, he's a dandy," Burke declared.

Smiling faintly, the Magician lifted the glass, drained it and said huskily, "That stuff would burn a hole through an anvil."

"Yeah, I know," Burke cackled gleefully. "Ain't it somethin'?"

"It's something, all right," Kale agreed, dropping a coin on the bar. He went through a wide doorway and into a narrow dining room where an Indian woman was just laying out plates full of deer stew before the passengers. Kale took a seat beside the young woman, nodded cordially and, when his meal was placed before him, began eating without preamble.

Hays came in and went into the kitchen, where he filled a plate from a large iron pot, and returning to the dining room, sat down next to the drummer and began eating.

The woman looked up then and asked, "Mr. Hays, how much longer before we reach Benson?"

"If we're lucky and don't lose a wheel, or Injuns don't shoot us up, or maybe outlaws hit us, we should arrive there by about one in the morning, Miss O'Brien," Hays assured her.

The gambler smiled faintly and observed, "Mr. Hays certainly likes looking on the bright side," and went back to his meal.

The drummer, having cleaned his plate, called, "Hey, you," to the Indian woman and held up his plate. She came and took it and returned in a few moments with it heaping again. As the drummer dug in, Miss O'Brien looked on with an expression of disapproval showing plainly on her face.

Burke came in from the bar and, settling at one end of the table, looked at the cavalry officer, and asked, "Colonel Bedlam, sir, I've heard rumors that some of the red stick chiefs are making war talk?"

The tall, gray-haired officer looked up, finished chewing and said quietly, "There has been some talk, but with the 'Paches one should consider they are always at war. It's safer that way."

"Have you had patrols out north of here?" Burke inquired.

"Yes, Mr. Burke, we have," Bedlam said. "Our scouts have seen tracks of small parties. We have no way of knowing whether they are war parties or hunting parties."

At that moment someone came into the bar, his spurs ringing a bell-like announcement. Burke rose looking puzzled, for very few lone travelers rode this land.

Stepping through the door, he found a tall young man wearing a gray hat and dressed in working ranch clothes leaning on the bar. At his hip dangled a .44, its butt slanted slightly forward, the tip of the holster that held it tied to the man's chap-clad leg. He was a pleasant enough appearing man and, nodding, Burke rounded the bar and stood, hands on the plank, waiting for the stranger's order.

"Whiskey," the man said and Burke met his eyes and they held nothing. Turning quickly, he found a glass, went through the dust-cleaning ritual and placed it before the cold-eyed man and filled it.

Lifting the drink with his left hand, he said, "To a fast horse, a faster woman and a damn fast draw," and tilted and drained it.

Staring at the stranger's right hand, Burke didn't know what to make of it. A strange-looking leather glove covered the hand. Crossed straps were attached to the back of it and they in turn wrapped around the man's wrist. It was an odd contraption and, in the blistering summer heat of the San Pedro River country, had to be uncomfortable.

About to ask about the glove, Burke was interrupted by the appearance of the Colonel and Kale.

Moving up to the bar, Bedlam glanced at the man with the glove and then said, "You seem to be a man who gets around, Mr. Torrey," and he extended a hand and the man called Torrey shook it.

At the mention of the name Torrey, the Magician faltered in his stride, then proceeded to the bar and, leaning on it, asked for whiskey, not looking at the stranger.

Burke stared at Torrey and said quietly, "Vent Torrey . . . Leatherhand. I should have known."

Vent smiled and nodding at Bedlam, said, "Give the Colonel here a drink," and then speaking to the gambler, asked, "How about you, sir. Will you join us?"

Kale turned slowly and looked at Vent and then nodded, accepted his drink and looked away.

Vent Torrey was a man who had put down his share of men. No one knew for sure how many he had killed, but the figure had been put at over twenty-five and some said as high as forty men had died before his blazing .44. He was a professional and a widely known professional. Now small bells of alarm began ringing in his head as he watched

Kale, while seemingly engaged in idle conversation with Bedlam.

Burke turned to Kale and said, "Mr. Kale, this here's Mr. Vent Torrey. They call him Leatherhand," and when Kale looked at Vent and nodded, Burke added, "Mr. Kale's known around Arizona as the Magician. Does some right fancy tricks."

Smiling faintly, Vent looked at Kale and said, "I've heard of you. You've left your mark around. In fact, a feller could follow your trail by the graves you've filled."

Kale, his face expressionless, observed, "You've put a few down yourself, so I've heard."

Hays came in and glanced at Vent and said, "Gentlemen, stage leaves in five minutes. Them that's not on it gets left behind," and went outside.

"You come in from the south?" Bedlam asked.

"East," Vent said.

Bedlam stared at him. "Hell, man, that's Apache country out there. Where the devil did you start from?"

"Safford," Vent said noncommittally.

Miss O'Brien came through the bar, glanced at Vent, smiled vaguely, and went outside, followed by the drummer and the man called Wolf. Watching him pass, Vent glanced at Burke and inquired, "Ain't that Wolf just went out?"

"That's him all right," Burke replied.

"You know him, Vent?" Bedlam asked.

"Heard of him," was all he said then shaking the Colonel's hand, told him, "probably run onto you again, sir," and, nodding at Burke, dropped a silver dollar on the bar to pay for the drinks and stepped outside.

Ah Kee came out behind Vent, looked at him and smiled his inscrutable smile and spoke softly to the drummer, who looked around and answered. The two mounted the coach from the off side as Hays assisted Miss O'Brien.

7

Vent stood beside the big Appaloosa while the animal sucked up water from a windmill-fed horse trough and watched Hays shout his team into a high lope south, a streamer of dust flagging its passing as it rocked from view around the corner of a low hill.

Burke came out and watched the coach disappear. Glancing at Vent, he stood as if undecided, then came over and looked at the Appaloosa and remarked, "That's one hell of a horse you got there."

"I've had him for a long time," Vent said.

"You riding south, are you?"

Vent looked at him for a moment then said, "I reckon," and stepped into the saddle. Gigging up the big horse, he put him to the stage road, waving casually at Burke as he passed.

An hour south of the station he heard faint shots and pulled in the horse, holding him still in the middle of the road. Nothing happened for a long breath then faintly, two more shots sounded and Vent put spurs to the horse and shot away down the road, his eyes searching the slopes and rocks as he whipped around each swinging turn. He found the stage half an hour later. It stood in the middle of the road, its off-wheel horse lying dead in the traces while the rest of the team, having exhausted themselves in an attempt to kick their way free of the stage, stood trembling and blowing. When they heard the Appaloosa approach, they walled their eyes and snorted, but Vent spoke quietly to them and the sound of a human voice had its soothing effect.

Without dismounting, Vent very carefully rode around the stage, his eyes checking the ground for sign, then he pulled his rifle from its scabbard and jacking a shell into the chamber, rode cautiously to the stage and peered inside through an open door. There was blood on the floor and one door, and an officer's glove lay abandoned on a seat. There was no sign of the passengers.

Vent walked slowly around the stage, this time on foot, and between watching the surrounding hills and checking for sign, he made a complete tour and in doing so put a picture together. A band of at least ten riders had come off the bank from the east at a lunge and probably shot the lead horse immediately, bringing the stage to a grinding halt and shaking up the passengers so badly that by the time they had untangled themselves, they were under the riders' guns. In spite of this, someone had fired shots and had been wounded for his efforts. Vent was certain that if he had been killed here, they would have left the body for the buzzards.

The sign led him to the south for fifty feet and it was here he saw where the horses had climbed from the road and struck out in a northeasterly direction.

Walking back to the coach, he stood there for a long moment then a voice from behind him said harshly, "Just stand right there, mister, and don't try to use that rifle."

"Mr. Hays, do you mind if I turn around?" Vent asked.

"Go ahead, turn around," the driver growled.

Slowly, so as not to invite a nervous shot, Vent turned full around and looked at Hays, who was leaning against the side of the coach, his left shoulder and side smeared with blood.

Nodding at him, Vent said, "I'm the feller was at Riverside Station . . . Name's Vent Torrey . . ."

Hays nodded. "Yeah, you're the gent they call Leatherhand. Why you here?"

"Heading south. Heard the shots and came on to investigate. What happened to your passengers?"

Looking down at the shotgun he held Hays said, "Aw hell," and lowered it and walked carefully to the door of the stage and eased himself painfully to the step. Looking up at Vent he shook his head. "They hit us a-runnin' and nailed me first off. I went over the side and landed down the bank there," and he raised his chin and then flinched.

"Who were they?"

"Mixed bunch," Hays said. "Looked like Apaches and half a dozen white men."

"Commancheros," Vent spoke softly.

"Maybe, mabye not," Hays grunted and then lay his head back against the side of the coach and observed, "Me, I'm getting too damn old for this . . . Hand me down the water jug, will you?"

Vent climbed up and dug out a canteen from the boot and handed it to Hays and watched as he gulped at the water greedily.

"How come they didn't finish you off?" Vent asked.

"Left me for dead," Hays said. "Heard one of 'em tell another to forget me, that when he shot a man he stayed shot."

"Best get you back to Riverside," and Vent went and cut out the dead horse and repaired the harness, then came to Hays and said, "Let me give you a hand inside."

"Riverside's too damn far," Hays grunted. "Tell Monger's ranch is about three miles south. Best make for there. His missus, she's pretty fair at doctorin'."

Nodding, Vent tied the Appaloosa to the rear of the coach and then helped Hays inside and made sure he was comfortable and climbed to the box. When he drove the stage up in front of Monger's place a tall, stoop-shouldered rancher came from the barn and seeing who his visitor was, shouted to the house and hurried over in time to help Vent lift Hays, who had passed out, from the coach. Neither man spoke as they carried the old man inside and at Mrs. Monger's directions, placed him in a spare bedroom.

Glancing incuriously at Vent, she said, "Hot water, Tell, and that old sheet I put away for bandages."

Vent walked outside and untied the Appaloosa and stepped into the saddle and then Monger came to the door and looked at him and said, "You going somewhere?"

Vent nodded. "Figure to see if I can track the fellers that hit that stage. They took away seven passengers, including a woman."

"Wait," Monger ordered and walked to the bunkhouse and came out again followed by a lean, rangy young man who was strapping two shell belts around his waist while holding a Winchester under his arm. Monger shouted to somebody at the barn, ordering him to saddle two fast horses then, nodding at Vent, said, "This here's Harp Denton. He's some handy at tracking," and he waited for Vent to identify himself.

Vent nodded and said, "Name's Vent Torrey, from Missouri and Colorado."

Monger's eyes narrowed and Denton openly stared as both men seemed to take notice of Vent's peculiar glove at the same time.

"Leatherhand, by God," Monger murmured.

A cowboy came riding from the barn on a big, raw-boned bay and leading a tough-looking grulla. Handing the reins to Denton, he glanced at Monger inquiringly.

"Bill, you ride like hell for Benson. Get hold of the law down there and tell them the Oracle-to-Benson stage's been hit by outlaws. They've grabbed all seven passengers . . . and be sure and let them know one of the passengers is a woman."

The cowboy whistled and then whirled the big horse and slamming the hooks to him, shot out of the yard and hit the stage road south, a long coil of dust marking his passage as he rode full out for Benson.

"Harp, you go along with Mr. Torrey," Monger ordered. "He's gonna try and track these fellers. Now hear me; don't you go getting yourself killed. You listen to Mr.

11

Torrey. He's an old hand at this. If you get plugged maw'll never forgive us.''

Denton grinned a lopsided grin and observed, ''Can't have that. I'll be careful,'' and waving, followed Vent from the yard at a hard lope.

They hit the kidnappers' tracks at the place where they left the road and were still trailing them when darkness interrupted them. Looking at Denton, who had proved almost as good a tracker as Vent, he said, ''Reckon we best make camp. Those fellers ain't going anywhere at night. Not with seven captives.''

Vent went over the ground carefully until he found an overhanging cliff facing west and, gathering up a handful of wood, soon had a small fire going. While Denton brewed coffee, Vent filled his hat from a large waterbag suspended from behind his cantleboard and allowed the Appaloosa a drink, then did the same for the grulla. Leading them down into a low draw, he fed each a handful of grain from his saddlebags and then staked out the grulla and turned the Appaloosa free.

Watching him in the fast-fading light, Denton waited until he returned to the fire then, handing him a cup of coffee, asked, ''Ain't you afraid that critter will run off and leave you afoot?''

''Nope. He'll not leave me. Had him for several years. He don't have no home except where I'm at.''

Denton placed a frying pan in the glowing coals and decorated it with several large strips of bacon cut from a slab he had dug out of his saddlebags.

Explaining, he said, ''Just got back from a two-day ride north looking for strays along the San Pedro. Had quite a bit of grub left and plenty of water and grain. We can use mine in the morning.''

Vent ate bacon and three-day old biscuits and carefully examined his young companion. He saw a lean, hard-bitten man of about twenty-five, whose face showed he had ridden some tough country in his life, a fact that didn't surprise Vent for he knew that many boys as young as sixteen became men overnight in this hard country.

Apparently aware of Vent's scrutiny, Denton glanced at him and grinned his lopsided grin and said, "You've got one hell of a rep in this country, Mr. Torrey."

"So I'm told . . ."

"Bother you?"

Vent smiled. "Not really. Feller is what he becomes and that's usually the result of where he's been in the past and what he's done there. Me, I fell into pistol fighting by accident and family circumstances."

Denton nodded. "I've heard the story of you and the Hawks family; how you and them feuded back and forth for years. Any truth in that?"

"Well, I guess we did our share of killing back in Missouri," Vent admitted. "Hawks and Torreys always been at each other. Now they's just two of us left; me and old man Hawks."

"They say you folks built your own cemeteries," Denton said.

"I reckon we did, but then most of us was still a gleam in our daddy's eye long after the feud started. All we knowed was a Hawks was fair game and all the Hawks knowed was that a Torrey was a fair target."

Staring at Vent curiously, Denton asked, "How many went down in that feud?"

"More than 500," Vent said calmly and Denton stared at him, then said softly, "My God!"

Vent smiled. "You have to remember, Harp, the damn feud ran on for over seventy years."

"Maybe this here's not a good question, but I'm gonna ask it anyway." Denton said slowly. "How old were you when you killed your first Hawks?"

"About twelve years old," Vent said and rose and walked into the night.

The gray-eyed woman sat with her back against a rock and watched the leader of the gang of kidnappers who had pulled her from the stage along with the other passengers go about setting up camp. He was very methodical and very thorough. There were twelve of them, four Apaches and eight white men. The Apaches ignored her, but the white men kept staring at her. When she caught one of their eyes, what she saw there frightened her.

Now she carefully examined this man who had captured the entire passenger list from a stagecoach. He was of medium build, but possessed wide shoulders and heavily muscled arms. His hands, she noted, were long and slim and more suited to playing the piano than handling guns, although she had to admit that he was very good. He had given the drummer a demonstration when the fat man said something the leader didn't like. He had suddenly drawn a gun and leveled it at the drummer, who merely gazed into the bore and waited.

The leader wore his hair down to his shoulders and had a thin, almost aristocratic face, bisected by a patrician nose. His mouth was wide and he smiled often, which surprised her, for she found it hard to realize that men bent on such a grim task would have time or the inclination for levity.

She had heard several of the men refer to the leader as Captain Samuels. He did wear a cavalry officer's hat and a pair of blue pants undoubtedly issued by the Union. However, Colonel Bedlam, who now sat leaning against a small tree across the fire from her with his hands and feet tied, acted as if Samuels did not exist and most certainly had never served honorably in the Union.

The rest of the white men with Samuels were a wild-looking lot. Three of them wore beards that were badly in need of trimming. Long hair seemed to predominate. Their clothing was nondescript to the extreme. One man wore a pair of butternut trousers, which indicated he was probably a Confederate soldier at one time and another had on chaps, a fancy pair of spurs with huge Mexican rowels, a wide-brimmed hat and a blue neckerchief. The man who was second-in-command was referred to by the others as Sergeant MacIntosh and they followed his orders as quickly as they did Samuels's. The Apaches wore their usual white leggings, white skirtlike breechcloths and colored shirts. Each wore a handkerchief twisted around his head to keep his long black hair from getting in the way. They carried Spencer single shot rifles and wore gunbelts with holstered Frontier Model Colt .45 Army-issue handguns.

Samuels had sent two of them on their back trail and the other two were hidden in strategic locations east of the encampment.

Ah Kee, his face inscrutable, had been tied and placed with his back to a sandstone bank that backed up the camp and effectively hid the fire from prying eyes. Now he watched the outlaws with what appeared to be idle interest.

The man called Wolf looked naked without his pistols. He was tied hand and foot and lay near the bank with his hat over his eyes, apparently sleeping. Beside him the drummer, who had said his name was Mike Overly, sat with his knees bent and his head down, also apparently asleep. The girl doubted these men knew her relationship to Wolf.

She looked at Colonel Bedlam and he smiled faintly and winked.

The Magician was sitting five feet to her right. They had put a pair of Army-issue handcuffs on him rather than tie him, but it was obvious Samuels knew him and his reputation. One of the outlaws sat with a rifle trained on the dark-eyed gambler.

Samuels came around the fire and bowing to her, said, "Now, Miss O'Brien, I certainly hope you aren't too uncomfortable."

Looking up at him, her face suddenly flushed with embarrassment, she asked in a low voice, "Would it be possible . . . for me to have a few minutes by myself. I give my word I won't try to run away?"

"Certainly," Samuels said and bent and untied her hands, then called to one of his men. "Burt, you escort this lady to a place where she can be alone, and mind you, leave her to herself for at least five minutes. If she tries to run away, shoot her."

He nodded and said not unkindly, "This way, miss," and led her from the camp and to a narrow draw that apparently dead-ended at its upper reaches. Pointing, he said, "Down there, miss, but mind you, watch for rattlers. This here country is full of them."

Nodding, she walked down the gentle slope and around the first bend, then lifted her skirts and quickly relieved herself and stood up, adjusting her clothes and wondering where the Apaches were. Probably spying on me, she thought and suddenly it didn't make much difference. She was sure that sooner or later these men would decide to rape her. Thinking about it, she found tears in her eyes, and she suddenly wondered why her father put her in this dangerous position. He possessed the power to have sent a military escort with her so why didn't he, she wondered.

"Miss, you all right?" her guard called, and she climbed the slope and thanking him for being a gentleman, allowed him to return her to the camp. She was again tied and left leaning against the rock.

Food was served to the prisoners one at a time and then suddenly it was dark and Samuels was handing out blankets,

16

which each prisoner was allowed to wrap himself in. When the outlaw distributing them came to Kale, Samuels said, "Not him, at least he's not to cover his hands. Put it over his lower body, but make sure his hands stay in plain sight."

Miss O'Brien slept fitfully. When she finally awoke, stiff and sore in every muscle and bone of her body, she glanced to where the Magician had been and there was only a blanket there. His guard, too, was gone as if vanished into thin air. When Samuels awoke and discovered Kale missing, Miss O'Brien saw a different side of his personality. Standing spraddle-legged before the prisoners, hands on hips, he said coldly, "It appears Mr. Kale no longer desired our company. He has vanished, along with the guard, whose job it was to watch him. I'm sure we will find that unfortunate man lying nearby with his throat cut."

Overly looked at Bedlam, who merely watched Samuels and waited. Ah Kee stared into infinity. Wolf smiled faintly and attempted to roll a cigarette with his hands tied.

"You may think that by escaping Mr. Kale will enhance your chances for rescue," Samuels said. "On the contrary. He may have written your death warrant. If pursuers get too close, we'll be forced to rid ourselves of unwanted witnesses . . ."

Miss O'Brien stared at him. "You mean, you'd murder us all?"

Looking at her he said, "Not all Miss, O'Brien. You, I'll let live. I can get half a dozen good horses from the Apaches for you."

"That's monstrous," she snapped, glaring at him.

"Would you rather I handed you over to my men?" he asked and his voice was silky soft.

Overly spoke then, observing, "No use talking to a border thief, Miss O'Brien . . . even one traveling under the guise of a gentleman. They have no conscience or they wouldn't be doing what they're doing.''

Without looking at Overly, Samuels snapped, ''Sergeant, kick that man in the face,'' and the sergeant, who was standing five feet from Overly, whirled and slammed a heavy boot into the drummer's face, crushing his lips and breaking his nose. The blow knocked him sideways and he lay there for a moment then painfully sat up and said distinctly, ''Samuels, you better kill us because if you don't, I'll see you and the rest of this desert rabble swinging from a gibbet.''

Still not looking at Overly, Samuels shouted, ''Sergeant, kick him again,'' and as the sergeant started to comply, Miss O'Brien shouted, ''No! Don't . . . do that . . .''

The sergeant stopped, glanced at the captain and waited. Overly, his arms covering his face, waited stoically for the blow.

Walking over to Overly, Samuels looked at him for the first time. ''Mr. Drummer, you've had a reprieve, but the next time you open your fat face, I'll have you hanged and the rest of these folks can watch you kick. You understand?''

Overly nodded and Samuels jerked his head and the sergeant walked to the fire and poured himself a cup of coffee.

Samuels was about to speak again when one of the men came from a shallow canyon to the west and said, ''Captain, I found Slade. He's down there. Deader than a nit. Throat cut . . . The Apaches are also gone . . .''

Samuels stared at him. ''What the hell you mean, they're gone?''

''Just that, sir. They're gone. I looked all over down there. Found where they spent the night, but they're not there now.''

Turning to one of the other outlaws, Samuels snapped, ''Up on the hill. Check those boys I sent east.''

Half an hour later as Samuels sat brooding and drinking coffee, the man returned and shook his head. "Gone, sir," he said.

"The Magician?" he asked.

"No sign out there, sir," the man said uneasily. It was obvious he did not like this.

Miss O'Brien could almost see Samuels's brain working as he said softly, "Even the Magician couldn't out-fox those boys. They were the best. Means somebody else has bought into this game," and then a shot slammed the morning apart and one of the men screamed, jerked upright and, mouth pouring blood, held out a futile hand of protest, then suddenly collapsed into the fire and did not move.

Samuels's men were well trained. They disappeared to cover within seconds of the shot and looking around, Miss O'Brien found herself and her fellow prisoners apparently alone. Deciding now was a good time to run, she started to rise, but Bedlam said sharply, "Don't," and she settled back against her rock and waited.

"Dorton, get up on the high ground above us and see if you can spot him," Samuels ordered.

Miss O'Brien watched as one of the outlaws began crawling up a narrow cut that led to the low hill above the encampment as the others stayed hidden. He had just reached the top when the rifle boomed again, its heavy slug tearing through the outlaw's body and sending him toppling end over end back down the slope and into the encampment, where he came to rest against Bedlam's ankles.

The colonel did not move.

Suddenly Samuels shouted, "You, out there. The next shot you fire I'm going to match it with a shot into one of the prisoners. I'll start with the colonel . . ."

Silence greeted this sally.

The colonel spoke then. "You always were an idiot, Samuels, even when I served with you at Appomattox. Whoever's out there isn't interested in us. He's after you and your people."

Samuels crawled into view from behind a boulder and rifle in hand, stared at Bedlam. "Now what the hell is that supposed to mean?"

"Simple. It isn't the Magician. I know the man. By now he'll be halfway back to Riverside. And he hasn't had time to fetch help. Besides, if he did get help, you'd be facing a large posse out there, one whose only interest would be to win our release. They wouldn't fire on this camp for fear you'd start killing prisoners."

"Then who the hell's out there?" Samuels shouted.

Bedlam shook his head. "I'm as puzzled as you are, Captain."

So they remained pinned down for almost an hour, then Samuels, tired of lying cramped and thirsty, looked around and decided to chance making a try for the hidden rifleman.

"Burt, you and Clayt see if you can sneak up on that feller," he ordered. The two men hesitated then slipped away through the brush.

A slow half hour crept by, then one of the men stood up three hundred feet from the camp and called, "Captain, I found the spot," and Samuels rose, walked out and had his look and returned to the fire, where he ordered camp struck.

"No food, Captain?" Miss O'Brien asked.

Looking around at his depleted command, Samuels said, "No time, Miss O'Brien. I'm sorry. You'll just have to bear with the rest of us," and he mounted and led the small cavalcade away. Samuel's men were now outnumbered by their prisoners.

As they traveled, Clayt and Burt ranged on the right and left as flankers. Each carried his rifle across his saddle.

Samuels kept his rifle butt down against his thigh. The sergeant rode a hundred yards in front of the group, his sharp eyes missing nothing.

They traveled steadily for three hours, then Samuels called a halt and the outriders came in.

Ordering his prisoners to dismount, Samuels stepped down, then, looking at his depleted command, his face turned suddenly wild and he drew his gun and snarled, ''Damned if I don't kill you all!''

The sergeant restrained him and, after a brief struggle, the captain subsided, lowering the hammer on his gun and staring around as if dazed.

Then the hidden rifleman fired again and Burt screamed, spun around and collapsed as Bedlam's horse reared, whirled and dashed into the scrub. Samuels, cursing wildly, fired a shot at the colonel and missed.

''He's up on top of that cliff,'' MacIntosh shouted and loosed five rapid shots from his rifle. Miss O'Brien could hear the bullets whine away as they struck the rocks above them, but she was sure none had hit their mark.

Clayt, hunkered down behind a large boulder, said, ''Captain, whoever that feller is, he can damn sure shoot.''

''Idiot,'' Samuels mumbled.

Again they were pinned down for more than half an hour until finally Samuels decided to chance moving. Crouching, he ran from his hiding place to a stand of palo verde growing just beneath the overhanging cliff and dodged from sight. Twenty minutes later he stood up on top of the cliff and called down, ''Clayt, get those folks on the horses and bring them around the south side of this cliff. I'll meet you down there.''

Clayt stood up and a shot smashed out. The outlaw took the round just to the left of his shirt pocket, shouted, ''Ouch!'' and spun around and ran lumberingly off to the south, his hands clutching his wound. While the prisoners stared, he stopped, turned around and looking at them, said distinctly, "I wouldn't have done you a hurt," and pitched on his face, dead.

Staring at the body, the sergeant suddenly turned and ran.

Then, Bedlam appeared from behind some bushes and, racing into the camp, retrieved his pistol and saber from the packhorse and, quickly cutting the others free, stood by while they armed themselves.

High on the cliff, Samuels stood and watched his prisoners ride away to the west. Once Miss O'Brien looked back and saw him still standing there.

Wolf rode alongside her and asked, "You all right, ma'am?"

"I'm fine," she said, and thought, that is, I will be once I've slept around the clock and had something to eat and a bath.

Samuels cursed when he saw that the prisoners were taking all the horses, including his own. Finally, he made his way down from the cliff and to the camping area, where he stripped the two dead outlaws' guns from them and gathered up enough food to fill a pair of saddlebags. They had left two of the smaller canteens behind and for that he was grateful, deciding it must have been the colonel who showed him such consideration.

Loaded down like a packhorse he turned and walked south around the base of the rocky escarpment and then struck out due east. As he passed around the base of the cliff, the sergeant fell in behind him. Neither said a word.

The man known as the Magician reached the stage road in three days. He had traveled the last twenty-four hours dry and now, as he stood in the dust and gazed ruefully down at his ruined boots, he wasn't sure which he missed the most; a decent pair of boots or a canteen of water. Shrugging, he crossed the road and made his way down to the San Pedro River, where he drank sparingly, filled his stolen canteens and then set about removing his boots and lowering his feet into the cool water. He was sitting, thinking about a large, rare steak, when a slight sound yanked him back to reality and the fact he was in the middle of Apache country. Casually standing up he turned and stretched and then suddenly his hands were full of guns and he had dropped behind a down log and leveled the weapons at a nearby bush.

"Come to hell outa there," he ordered.

A tall young man strolled from the brush leading an Appaloosa horse. "Little sudden there, ain't you, Kale?"

Kale stood up and holstered his gun and turned back to the river and reimmersed his feet, ignoring his visitor.

Grinning, Vent Torrey led the Appaloosa downstream and allowed him to drink and then drank himself, filling his canteens first.

Kale glanced at him and asked, "That you doing all the shooting east of here?"

"As a matter of fact, it was," Vent said, sitting down with his back against a tree while his horse cropped the rich river bottom grass.

"Get them all?"

"All but Captain Samuels and the second-in-command," Vent nodded.

"And the prisoners?"

"Should just about be arriving at Riverside Station," Vent told him and dug out the makings and rolled a cigarette, then extended the sack to Kale, who shook his head and instead conjured up a cigar, materialized a small penknife and carefully cut away the end of the smoke and stuck it between his teeth. His finger suddenly blossomed flame

23

and he casually lit the cigar then offered Vent a light. Vent accepted without comment or surprise.

"Heard from Owney Sharp lately?" Kale inquired.

"He's dealing faro at Denver," Vent replied, watching the Magician pull his tattered socks back on blistered feet and shove them into his ruined boots.

"Damned country's rough on boots," he said.

Vent rose and walked to his horse and, unstrapping a saddlebag, dug out a pair of moccasins and tossed them to Kale.

"Try these," he said and Kale removed his boots and gratefully slipped on the moccasins.

Standing up, he looked at the boots sourly, then heaved them out into the river and said, "Guess I better head for Riverside."

"I brought one of those Apache's horses if you don't mind riding an Injun pony," Vent invited.

Kale stared at him. "Mr. Torrey, you don't happen to have a rare steak on you, do you?"

"Afraid not, but they tell me that Injun gal at the Riverside Station can cook up dandy deer steaks."

Nodding, Kale said, "Lead off," and followed Vent into the trees where he found a horse tied.

"Might ought to water him," Vent suggested, then waited until Kale rode the animal to the river, allowed him to drink and rode him back. Vent gigged the Appaloosa up onto the stage road and headed north.

They arrived at the station just as the sun dropped behind the dry sandstone cliffs west of the river and found the prisoners inside sitting at the big dining room table eating huge plates of stew.

When Kale and Vent walked in and leaned against the bar, Bull Burke came around the end of the plank and nodding, said, "See you made her, Mr. Kale."

"I made it," Kale agreed and, accepting the full glass

of whiskey gratefully, dumped it down his throat with a flick of the wrist.

"You fellers couldn't have heard but the northbound came through here yesterday and Ord Danbury said they was a hell of a shootout down in Tombstone. Seems as how the Earp brothers and Doc Holliday shot the hell outen the McLowry brothers and Billy Clanton. Killed the three of 'em dead as Adam's off ox."

"How'd the Earps come out?" Vent asked.

"Virgil got hit in the leg and Morgan took a round in the back," Burke said. "That damned Ike Clanton, he ran off. Wouldn't fight. Yeller pup . . ."

Colonel Bedlam came into the bar. Seeing Vent and Kale, he walked over and grinned. "Mr. Torrey, you do get around."

"Glad to see you're all right, colonel," Vent said.

"I have an old soldier's hunch that we wouldn't be here if it wasn't for you," Bedlam remarked.

"They tell you why they did it?" Vent asked.

"That's the odd thing about this," Bedlam looked puzzled as Burke set him up a glass and filled it with whiskey. "They just grabbed us. Never told us where they were taking us or why."

Turning to Burke, Vent asked, "How'd Hays make out?"

"Monger's wife patched him up and I sent him back north on the Oracle run. He was hurting, but he'll make her."

Vent glanced up then and nudged Kale, who was looking in the mirror watching a man who had just stepped through the door and was standing with his hand on his gun looking around.

"Know him?" Vent asked.

"Sheriff of Pima County. Name's Phillip Rodriguez," Kale said.

Then the sheriff came down the room and nodding at Burke, said, "Mr. Burke, we haven't found hide nor hair of your passengers and we been all over them hills to the east," then he glanced at Vent and Kale and said, "Did find several dead men, including four Apaches."

"Yep, somebody picked 'em off one by one, according to the passengers," and Burke jerked a thumb toward the dining room and said, "they're in there catching up on lost meals."

Rodriguez stared at him. "Well, I'll be damned," he said and walked into the dining room.

Chapter II

A dry wind came off 5,470 foot Sierra del Humo, pushing the dust from a long column of horsemen and pack animals south where it flattened out against the base of the narrow cliffs on each side of the mountain cut the mounted men were passing through.

The grizzled oldster riding the big buckskin out in front of the main column lifted his mutilated right hand and fumbled his neckerchief up to cover the lower half of his face, leaving only the icy gleam of washed-out blue eyes showing. He sat ramrod straight in the saddle, his shoulders back and square and his head up and alert in spite of the dust-carrying winds of the pass. He wore heavy bullhide chaps, a scratched and ripped cowhide vest that had seen better days and a pair of bronc-heeled boots adorned with Mexican spurs. As he rode the tiny bells on each rowel gave off a musical note, an incongrous addition to the accoutrements of a man who looked as if he had been carved from a piece of granite.

On his left hip rode a .45 Colt Peacemaker, its bone handles high in the holster. Beneath his right leg a 38.40 rifle filled a scarred leather scabbard. The rest of his gear was as badly used. His saddle was an old centerfire rig out of Texas, called a "bear trap" because of its high cantleboard. The make had trapped more than one man in a fall. The stirrups were oxbows and no bronc rider would use them because a man could easily shove his boot through them and wind up being dragged to death if he got bucked off.

None of this bothered the old man. He knew all about such gear, but did not fear being either bucked off or dragged.

As he rode stolidly along the canyon floor, his eyes never stopped checking the canyon walls and at each side canyon he slowed his horse and kept his hand close to his gun.

Halfway along the line of pack animals, a slat-thin Mexican wearing twin bandoliers of ammunition over his shoulders, and weighted down with two huge Dragoon pistols, gigged his horse with long-shanked spurs and galloped past half a dozen other Mexicans to pull in beside the old man.

Pushing his hat to the back of his head and ignoring the dust, the Mexican said, "Mr. Hawks, another mile and we'll be out of this canyon."

Hawks nodded.

Pulling his huge sombrero down snugly on his head, the Mexican pointed to a towering peak in the distance and said, "That is Mount Wrightson. We meet Captain Samuels five miles east of the base of that mountain."

Hawks looked at him and then asked, "Will he be there, this Captain Samuels?"

"Sí, he'll be there. He wants the guns . . ."

"And the money?"

The Mexican smiled. "He will have the *dinero* also, for he knows; no money, no guns."

Hawks grunted then asked again, although he had been assured of the fact once before, "It will be in gold eagles?"

"Sí, it will be in gold eagles," the Mexican assured him.

Nodding, Hawks rode on, ignoring the Mexican, who shrugged and turned back to dash along the column until he reached the halfway mark. Turning his horse, he assumed his original position and came on, humming to himself.

When they reached the mouth of the canyon, Hawks held up his hand and the column came to a stop. Riding forward, the old man broke into the open, pulled in his horse and sat and very carefully checked the terrain. He wasn't about to make a mistake now, not with $20,000 in guns riding on the mules behind him. Smiling inwardly, he thought, usually the guns are moved south instead of north, and wondered what the authorities at Fort Bowie would think if they were to seize the contraband he was carrying.

Certain that nothing waited for them out there, he turned and waved his hand and the column came on as Hawks led off at a sharp trot.

They camped that night in among a pile of huge boulders that formed a natural corral. There was a spring here and someone had taken the time to dig a sizable lake so that stock could be watered. Hawks figured the spring had probably watered its share of stolen horses, cattle and men on the run. Removing the packs, the Mexicans stacked them in among the rocks and then led the pack animals to the water and allowed them to drink. Once they had drank their fill, they were each given a bait of grain in a nosebag and left to munch contentedly. The saddle horses received the same treatment.

Two hours later Hawks finished cleaning up his plate of beans and bacon and gulped down the last of his coffee. Looking around he saw that the Mexicans, with the exception of Phillip Zermino, who was their leader, had stretched out and gone to sleep. Zermino sat and stared into the fire.

Hawks rose and walked out into the night, stopping behind a rock, where he relieved himself, then made a wide circle around the natural corral. The four men he had ordered out as guards were awake and alert. He knew they would remain alert, for this was Apache country and they had no desire to wind up with their throats cut. Returning to the fire, he sat down and glanced around. There were eight Mexicans and seven whites in the party. The white men were handling the first guard mount.

Zermino finally rose and, looking at Hawks, said, "I go to my blankets. Wake my men when it is their turn to guard," and he went to his silver-mounted saddle and removed a blanket from behind the cantleboard. Rolling up in it, he removed his hat and placed it over the saddle horn. He dropped his guns within easy reach near his head and, in what seemed moments, was asleep.

Hawks sat and allowed his head to sag on his chest, but a closer inspection would have revealed a pair of cold eyes watching Zermino and the other Mexicans.

The fire burned down by two in the morning and Hawks rose then and walking to Zermino, pulled his gun and, standing five feet from him, shot him in the head. The bullet struck with a solid thump and the Mexican, fatally wounded, jerked and then, legs tangled in his blanket, thrashed feebly. Before he had ceased kicking, the white men had shot the rest of the Mexicans. Those who did not die immediately Hawks quickly dispatched by simply slitting their throats with a large Bowie knife.

When the slaughter was over, they dragged the dead from the corral and dumped them over a bank into a rocky crevass. Back at camp Hawks looked at his *segundo*, T.J. Thorpe, and grinned.

"Reckon that'll save us part of the split," he said and sought his blankets.

Far to the north, two men sat in a buggy and held a quiet conversation. The bigger of the two, Arizona Senator Carl Burgess, raised his hand in a sharp gesture, then brought it down as if chopping wood and said, "Do you realize that if someone hadn't stepped in over there on the San Pedro, Rebecca could have been murdered, or worse yet, mistreated by that bunch of border ruffians?"

His companion, a swarthy, lean-faced man with bitter eyes and a slash of a mouth that never seemed to smile, nodded. "I know, Senator, and I'll take full responsibility for what happened."

Burgess looked sour. "A hell of a lot of good that would have done Rebecca."

"Everything worked out in the long run, didn't it?"

Quade Garvey waited for Burgess to reply, but instead the senator merely sat there thinking. Finally he spoke. "None of this makes sense. This fellow Samuels kidnaps everybody on that coach. Who was he after?"

Garvey was as mystified as was the senator. "They sure as hell weren't after Wolf. They couldn't have known he was our man hired to guard Rebecca . . ."

"And a damn poor job he did too," the senator said disgustedly.

"At least he didn't go off half-cocked and get her killed," Garvey replied.

"Were they after the Chinese, Ah Kee? They say he's worth a bundle, but hell, that may be talk . . ."

"Would they know he has been acting for us?" Garvey mused.

Burgess shook his head. "No one knows that anymore than they would know who Rebecca really is. Hell, she's been with her mother in Boston since she was a child. She's never been west.''

''What about the Magician? What the hell was he doing on that coach? Everybody knows he's a gun for hire. He doesn't have any allegiances.''

Burgess was far more concerned about the man who rescued the passengers. ''Bull Burke at the Riverside stage stop told Ira he was absolutely certain the man who killed Samuels's men was this gunfighter they call Leatherhand.''

Garvey looked toward the small stream winding its way through the valley where they sat under an oak tree and said softly, ''If that fellow's in this, he must be removed. He's probably the most dangerous man in Arizona right now.''

''One man?'' Burgess asked and raised an eyebrow.

''That's the problem,'' Garvey replied. ''He knows half a dozen of the top pistol fighters in the country and they are very loyal friends. Even killing him could be extremely dangerous to us, particularly if it brings in those men.''

''Who are they, anyway?'' Burgess asked.

Garvey, who had spent over ten years roaming the west, said, ''There's Owney Sharp, Cam Spencer, the Preacher and Arkie Chan.''

''That was the bunch that damned near destroyed the combine in Denver a couple of years ago, wasn't it?''

Garvey nodded. ''Sharp, Spencer and the Preacher were in on that, as well as some other top guns who got killed during the fight. . . . But they didn't damn near break them, they did it.''

''Where's this Leatherhand come from?'' Burgess asked.

''Missouri,'' Garvey replied.

''Which side was he on?''

''Neither. He was too young. . . . But I'll tell you this . . . his family and the Hawks family have been feuding for years . . .''

Burgess turned and stared at him. "You mean old Hitch Hawks?"

"Yes, Hitch Hawks. Leatherhand, his real name's Vent Torrey, is the lone male survivor of his family. He does have a sister out in Colorado, so they say."

"How many Hawks are left?" Burgess asked.

"Hitch Hawks is the last of his family."

"And we've got Hawks bringing in a load of guns," Burgess said.

Thinking about it, Garvey suddenly had an idea. "Hell, Senator, why don't we just let Hawks know Torrey's in this? Tell him he's on the opposite side. Hawks'll do his damndest to kill him and, if he succeeds, we're out of it. It's just the windup of one of the most famous feuds in Missouri history."

"When'll Hawks deliver the guns?"

Garvey thought a minute then said, "He's due to meet our people day after tomorrow but Samuels sure won't make it."

Picking up the reins, Burgess said, "Quade, you be there. Plant the seed," and he tapped the horses' rumps with the lines and drove from the grove toward Phoenix.

Far to the south the object of the senator's conversation was just putting his horse down a rock-strewn mountainside somewhere west of the mining town of Dragoon. He was tired and so was the Appaloosa. They had traveled all through the night, using the stars as a guide, and now, with first morning's light, were within gunshot distance of the small mining town.

As Vent turned his horse onto the main street and walked him to the first saloon, he hardly attracted a second glance, for he looked like any one of a thousand grub-line riders crisscrossing the west in those days. Pulling in at a water trough, Vent allowed the Appaloosa to drink, then rode on and stopped in front of the Miner's Delight Saloon.

Stepping down he loosed the cinch and, leaving the left hand stirrup hooked over the horn, walked inside where the thickness of the adobe walls pared the temperature by at least 25 degrees. The place held half a dozen customers, including four men playing poker at a table against a far wall. Glancing casually in that direction, he noted the black-clad, half-white, half-Chinese sitting with his back to the wall in the gunfighter's chair. Something passed between the two men, but anyone watching would have been hard pressed to put a finger on it.

Walking to the bar, Vent leaned against the mahogany and waited for the overweight, mustached bartender with the sleeve garters to waddle down and ask for his order.

"Whiskey," Vent said, then added, "Make it good whiskey. None of that damn rattlesnake stuff . . . I'll pay the difference."

Nodding, the bartender reached beneath the counter and selected a dust-covered bottle, brought it out and, turning away from Vent, blew the dust away and, choosing a clean glass from a rack on the back bar, carefully poured it full.

"That'll be a dollar," he said, watching Vent.

Digging in his chap pocket, Vent came up with several silver dollars, carefully placed two on the bar and asked, "How about food?"

"We got the hottest chili this side of Texas. Cost you a quarter. Also got stew made from everything but the cow's beller. Also a quarter."

Vent smiled. "I'll take a big bowl of that stew and another shot," and he tilted the glass and drank what he had and looked at the bartender and said, "Man, that's some scamper juice."

Grinning, the bartender refilled Vent's glass, picked up the two dollars and accepted an additional half dollar after

Vent said, "I'll probably get on the outside of two bowls of that stew."

Sitting at a table with his back to the wall, he dipped huge chunks of homemade bread into the stew and gulped it down, ignoring the other patrons. He was well into his second bowl when the door opened and a man wearing a star came in. Vent recognized him as the same lawman who had turned up at Riverside Station and tried to remember his name, but couldn't. The lawman was accompanied by four men with hardcase written all over them. Each sported a deputy's badge and all five, including the sheriff, toted two guns.

"Whiskey, Bobby, *amigo*," the sheriff ordered and Vent noticed the fat bartender did not dig out a special bottle for the lawman or his men.

Glass in hand, the sheriff turned and surveyed the room, his eyes finally lighting on the half-breed Chinese sitting in the poker game. Strolling back he nodded at one of the men, said, " 'Lo, Quinn," and the man named Quinn looked up and said, "Sheriff Rodriguez," and went back to studying his cards.

The dealer, a cold-eyed man wearing a small mustache and black clothes, looked so skinny Vent figured he'd have to stand twice to make a shadow.

Lifting his eyes from his cards, he asked, "What brings the sheriff of Pima County to Cochise County?"

"Duty, my gambling friend, duty," Rodriguez said.

"Wonder who's gonna wind up in boot hill now," the dealer mused, then inquired, "Cards, gentlemen?"

Apparently unaffected by the gambler's sally, Rodriguez continued to watch the game. The half-breed ignored him and when the call came for cards, took two.

Quinn grinned. "Mr. Chan, filling three of a kind is a tough bronc to ride and catching that fourth card is even tougher."

The half-breed called Chan grinned faintly then looked up and caught Rodriguez's gaze fastened on him. Vent, sitting behind the sheriff, noticed that when Chan's name was mentioned the man's back suddenly stiffened and his hands drifted down near his gun.

Watching him, Vent thought: Mister, you go for that thing and I swear I'll turn you into wolf meat.

Tossing off his whiskey, Rodriguez said quietly, "Lookin' for a feller calls himself Leatherhand. Any of you boys seen him around?"

Quinn looked up at the sheriff and observed, "You may wind up like the feller who grabbed holt the fifteen-foot rattler. . . . He had to have help to turn him loose. . . ."

Rodriguez grinned. "Just want to have a little talk with the man," and he tossed off his drink, looked at Chan again and turned down the room, jerking his chin at his deputies as he passed the bar and led them through the door.

"Long ways from home, that feller," one of the players observed.

Vent rose and nodded slightly at Chan, followed the sheriff out, wondering vaguely why the man had not recognized him. Out on the sidewalk he stopped short and then smiled and strolled to the Appaloosa, looked up at Rodriguez, and asked, "You wanted to see me, sheriff?"

The sheriff, sitting his horse, was alone, and Vent wondered where his deputies were.

"Mr. Torrey, you didn't stay around the Riverside Station long enough for me to ask some questions. . . . Like, were you the feller who shot those outlaws?"

Vent nodded. "Yep, I curled up a few, but the big honcho, that captain, went west; he and his right bower."

"You must be a pretty fair hand to take out four Apaches, let alone five experienced white men," Rodriguez observed, then Chan came through the door and seeing Vent with the sheriff, paused, nodded casually, and moved south along the sidewalk, a cigar stuck in his mouth at a jaunty angle.

"Know that feller?" Rodriguez asked.

"Looks vaguely familiar," Vent said, but then added, "most of them Chinese look alike."

"Like Mexicans, huh?" Rodriguez inquired.

"Like a lot of white men I know," Vent countered.

Rodriguez grinned. "Thanks for telling it to me straight. Those folks on that stage owe you a debt of gratitude," and he touched his hat and rode down the street.

Vent watched him until he hit the north end of town, where his men rode from a cross street and fell in on each side of him. Shrugging, Vent stepped aboard the Appy and rode south until he found Chan walking west down a narrow street. Turning, Vent followed him and saw the half-breed enter a small adobe at the end of the street. Looping his reins over a gatepost, Vent walked to the door and pushed his way inside where he found the half-breed pouring two drinks from a bottle of mescal.

"Arkie, how are you?" Vent asked, lifting the glass and pouring the fiery liquid down his throat. Lowering it, he said, "Damn, that stuff would burn the lining out of an Old Trilby stove."

"Good, ain't it?" Chan grinned.

Vent cleared his throat and looked around at the small house. There was a front room with a built-in Mexican-style fireplace, a narrow bedroom and a set of cupboards. It wasn't much.

"Looks like you ain't moved in here with a plan to stay," Vent observed.

"Just testing the water while I waited for you," Chan replied.

"By the looks of that stack of chips you had in front of you in that saloon, the water must be filled with gold around here," Vent observed.

"Hasn't been bad . . . You didn't ask me all the way out here from Bodie just to comment on my poker expertise. . . ."

Vent straddled a chair and leaning his chin on his crossed arms, said, "I brought you here because you once told me a feller name of Ah Kee, from Benson, was an uncle."

"He is, on my mother's side," and Vent smiled faintly at the sally.

"Seems he's involved in running guns up from Mexico," Vent said bluntly.

Chan shrugged. "I never knew Uncle Kee to pass up a fast dollar."

"Any idea why he might take up with a bunch of pro-slavers?"

Chan turned and stared at Vent from where he leaned against the fireplace, then shrugged again. "Same as before. Money."

"We got us a peculiar thing going on here," Vent said. "Seems a U.S. Senator named Carl Burgess is out to build himself an empire here in Arizona. He's thrown in with a bunch of Missouri border jumpers and killers on the dodge from federal marshals, who want them for everything from kicking somebody's dog to rape and murder during the war."

Chan nodded. "I know who Burgess is, but I've never heard he was pro-slavery."

"Neither has anybody else," Vent replied. "Seems as how we got two factions here in Arizona about to go to war with each other. Burgess heads up one and a gent by the name of Marcus Bell the other. . . ."

"Marcus Bell? Ain't he the man who damned near destroyed Freedom, Missouri, during the war?"

"That's him," Vent said. "Jayhawker, border guerrilla, murderer and hired assassin. A damned dangerous man."

38

"So what's this got to do with you . . . and me, if I decide to take a card?"

Vent rolled a cigarette and lit it. Blowing smoke, he looked at Chan and said quietly, "Hitch Hawks is working for Burgess."

Chan, like most people in the west, had heard the story of the Hawks-Torrey feud. He also knew that Vent and Hitch Hawks were the only male survivors. Now Hitch Hawks was in Arizona working for a pro-slavery senator who, if Vent had his facts correct, was about to tear the state apart.

"So," he said.

"Yep, he's running guns north from Mexico right now," Vent revealed.

"Usually they run guns into Mexico," Chan pointed out.

"Not when you got plans to build an army, you don't," Vent pointed out.

"You ain't telling me they plan to take over the whole state?"

"Not right away, but that's their ultimate aim. Right now them boys got it all put together to arm a small bunch of pro-slavers, mostly border riffraff and fellers that came to Arizona from Texas after the war, men from the 8th Texas Cavalry and the Texas Confederate Volunteers."

"Let me guess the rest," Chan said. "They got some kind of hideout in the desert around here and they plan to rob banks and stagecoaches for money. Maybe do a little cattle and horse stealing to feed and mount their men, all in the name of the Confederacy."

"Yep, that's about her. Never mind that the war's been over for many years."

"Some men need an excuse for robbing and killing," Chan observed.

"Friend of mine in Safford told me he heard a rumor

that Samuels had built a town off in the Pinaleno Mountains somewhere. Calls it Leesville, after General Lee. Got a bunch of them border killers hidin' out up there just waiting for the guns.''

''Who's picking them up . . . Your source tell you that?'' Chan asked, pouring them another drink.

Lifting the glass Vent walked to the window and looked out, then turned casually and winked and came back to the chair and sat down.

''Company?'' Chan asked.

Vent nodded. ''One of that Pima County sheriff's jack-leg deputies.''

''Shall I go haul him in here and see what he wants?''

Vent shook his head. ''Rodriguez probably ordered him to hang around. I doubt he's after anything in particular. Curious about you, more than likely.''

''How do you fit in all this?'' Chan asked.

''No official position,'' Vent replied. ''Just decided it might be a good time to finish some old business.''

''Hitch Hawks,'' Chan guessed.

''Should have killed that old man when I had the chance,'' Vent said. ''I had him at the muzzle of a shotgun out in Colorado once and let him walk away.''

Chan stared at him. ''Must have been young and foolish then.''

''Young, but hardly foolish. Just had a different code in them days.''

''So now what?''

''Guess maybe I'll see if I can't mess up mister Senator Burgess. . . . Wanta join in the festivities?''

Chan grinned. ''More like a funeral, but hell, I'm way ahead on the tables. Reckon I'll ride along just to watch you get plugged fulla holes.''

* * *

Hitch Hawks arrived east of Mount Wrightson and camped at the designated spot. He waited three days. When Samuels failed to show, he decided to pull out and find another buyer, take his profits and head back for Colorado, then three men rode into the camp, followed by T.J. Thorpe, who held them at gunpoint.

"Step down, boys," Thorpe ordered and when they were on the ground, told Hawks, "These fellers claim Samuels works for them. This gent here," and he jerked a thumb at the older of the three, "says his name is Quade Garvey."

Looking at Garvey, Hawks asked coldly, "What happened to Samuels?"

"We ain't sure. He grabbed all the passengers off the Oracle stage and headed east with them, but a gent they call Leatherhand got in his way. Killed his men. He's somewhere east of the San Pedro River. We've got people out looking for him. . . ."

At the name Leatherhand, Hawks's face closed in and he stared at Garvey, hearing little else he had to say. Holding up his hand, he said, "Hold it. You say Leatherhand stuck his nose in?"

"That's right. He's been marshaling over to Safford then we were told he suddenly quit the job and rode out. Nobody over there saw him again. He turned up at the Riverside Stage Station and when Samuels hit the coach, he went after him."

Hawks walked to the fire and absentmindedly poured a cup of coffee and stood up and drank the boiling brew as if it were ice water, then turned and said savagely, "Damn that bastard Torrey! I've waited too long to kill that damned snake-eyed son-of-a-bitch."

Garvey grinned and Thorpe nudged him with the gun and said quietly, "Be careful, my friend, if you wanta live to make it outa here," and the grin vanished from Garvey's face as he looked at the ground and stood perfectly still. The two men with him merely stared at Hawks, their faces unreadable.

"You bring the money for the merchandise?" Hawks asked.

"We've got it," Garvey said.

"Where?"

A small warning bell began to sound in Garvey's head as he looked at this hard old man and then stories of Hawks's past began to come back to him; of how the old man had fought for four long years in the Missouri Breaks, killing Union soldiers and border jumpers. Garvey knew the long story of the Hawks-Torrey feud and was depending on that information to get him away from here with the guns and his life.

"I hid it, Mr. Hawks," Garvey said.

Hawks looked up at him. "You hid it?"

"That's right."

"Why?" Hawks asked and he continued to stare at Garvey.

"Hell, Mr. Hawks, I had no idea what I'd find here," Garvey replied. "When we realized Samuels wasn't going to get here, we had to make a damn fast decision. It was decided I would come, but I was given strict orders not to actually bring the money into camp until I had seen the guns and received delivery."

Hawks shook his head. "You figure I'm gonna hand over $20,000 worth of guns just like that?"

"If you want the money you will," Garvey said and wondered how long he had to live. He had no delusions about this hard old man.

Hawks suddenly grinned a frosty grin and said, "All right. You tell me how you plan to work it."

Glancing down at Thorpe's gun, Garvey shook his head. "Not with a gun in my ribs, I don't."

42

Hawks looked at him with curiosity. "How the hell have you managed to live this long, Mr. Garvey?"

"I've always kept my word, for one thing," Garvey told him.

"So, how?"

Thorpe holstered his gun and the two men with Garvey, their own holsters conspicuously empty, went and helped themselves to coffee. Hawks knew them for what they were; hired guns and nothing more. They did not concern him. Garvey did.

Now Garvey came to the fire and picked up a tin cup and filled it from the big pot and, looking at Hawks, said, "You load up the mules and send this gentleman," and he nodded at Thorpe, "with us to pick up the money. He brings it back to you and we go on our way. Everybody's happy."

"What's to stop you from plugging Mr. Thorpe and leaving with the guns?" Hawks asked.

Garvey, gazing at Hawks over the edge of his cup, said quietly, "Mr. Hawks, I'm in this because I believe in slavery . . . or at least the right of choice in the matter. I'm a southerner. I fought as a colonel in the war. I now work for a United States senator, who believes the way I do. We are not interested in petty thievery, and believe me, Mr. Hawks, slickering you out of $20,000 in this game would be petty thievery. We, sir, are after a whole goddamn state."

Hawks thought that over then asked, "Where you from?"

"Georgia," Garvey said promptly.

"All right, Mr. Georgia Garvey, I'm going to do it your way," Hawks decided. "But they's one little thing you should maybe keep in mind; I never forget. Ask Vent Torrey. You euchre me outa this gun shipment, and you'll find me camped on your trail until I can put sights on you."

Thorpe glanced at Garvey and asked, "How you expect to get these here guns to where you're going?"

Garvey shrugged. "We'll get them there. That's our worry."

Thorpe shook his head. "Not hardly, Mr. Garvey. If the 'Paches hit you and wind up with them pieces, this whole frontier will go up in flame. Nobody will be safe. You're talking about taking over the state; hell, if the Injuns grab the guns, they'll take over the state. They's a feller called Geronimo who leads the Chiricahaus. He gets his small pleasures from stripping the skin off white folks an inch at a time and then spread-eagling them over a cholla and cutting off their eyelids so they can't close them. He's a right nice gent."

Hawks grinned and Garvey, looking at him, thought, he's probably enjoying this, and replied, "Mr. Thorpe, I'm well aware of what the Apaches would do if they got their hands on these guns. They'll not get them."

Hawks shrugged. "Your funeral," was all he said, then turned and ordered the mules loaded.

Before Garvey would accept the weapons, he insisted on examining each box, taking out a Spencer or Sharps and checking them over at random. Finally, Hawks, a wide grin on his grizzled faced, went to one mule and, pointing at a bulky object, said, "That's a Gatling on there, Mr. Garvey. The mount for it is on the grey mule. I'd suggest if the Injuns get too close . . . and you have the time . . . you unload that bugger and set her up. They ain't a tribe on the frontier who'll buck one of them things, not even the Apaches."

Garvey did not know about the Gatling. Apparently Samuels had been saving knowledge of it as a surprise.

Two days later, they crossed the stage road between Tombstone and St. David and headed northeast toward Dragoon, planning on swinging around the small mining settlement and striking for a rendezvous north of the Benson-El Paso stage road.

Samuels struggled up the slope of talus, his feet seemingly slipping backward two steps for every one he gained. It was hot enough to make a man's eyebrows crawl in this barren land and Samuels knew that if he didn't make it to Leesville before tomorrow noon, he probably wouldn't make it at all. When he finally reached the top of the slope, he sat down on a rock and looked around and thought, this is the way hell will be.

All around him grew catclaw, prickly pear, huge saguaro with thorny arms outstretched, octillo and bunches of mesquite. It was an unforgiving land and Samuels wondered vaguely why the hell he was here in the first place. He had planned to seize Colonel Bedlam and hold him for trial at Leesville, then hang him as a way of showing the world he meant business.

Delta Kale, the Magician, was another matter. Samuels's intelligence arm had also discovered the man was working for Marcus Bell. Samuels had planned to offer the gunfighter more money than the anti-slavers were paying and if Kale refused, kill him.

As to the girl, Rebecca O'Brien, she had merely been frosting on Samuels's cake. With her he figured he could bargain. She represented a pawn in the game in that the ex-captain knew she could be used to keep both a posse and the army off his back. The others seized in the raid on the stage meant nothing. The drummer, the man called Wolf and Ah Kee would have eventually been released or killed, whichever was the more expedient.

Looking down at his feet, he grimaced. The cavalry boots he wore were little more than rags. His britches from the knees down had been torn to shreds by the sharp-spined cactus that grew in profusion in this desolate land.

His lips were blistered as were the cheekbones of his face. He was hungry enough to eat the next rattler he found. He had risked detection . . . and he had no illusions about whether a posse was on his trail or not . . . by firing at a javelina, but had missed the elusive animal.

Standing up, he turned and sighting on a distant peak, he trudged east, his head down and his eyes half-closed against the glare of the sun.

He covered four miles by nightfall and knew he wasn't going to make it at that rate. He had consumed the last of his water two hours before sundown and already his throat felt as if it were swelling shut. Deciding to take advantage of the coolness of the evening, he went on, then suddenly stopped short, almost falling over a pincushion cactus. In a jagged cut running east from where he stood on a low ridge, a fire was sending off its faint glow. Samuels sat down quickly, not wanting to skyline himself until he knew who was down there. It could be the posse, some of his own men looking for him, or Apaches. Watching the fire for half an hour revealed nothing. It was too dark to see the dim figures moving around it and the blaze was too small to afford proper light. He decided to try and get closer.

Palming his .45 he worked his way down the slope until he came up behind several large rocks. Carefully raising his head, he stared and found himself looking at five Apaches gathered around a small fire tucked in under a rocky overhang. Probably the only place in the area it could be detected from was the top of the slope, Samuels guessed.

Counting up the odds, he hesitated. Five Apaches in anybody's book was four too many. He knew he could probably kill two of them before the remaining three faded into the desert, but then it would be a matter of time until they crept up on him and killed him in turn. No, he'd have to figure a way to get them all or sneak away from here. He did not want to do that, for down there was water, a horse and food.

Then one of the Indians rose from a squatting position, and grunting something to his companions, walked up the draw. He left his rifle behind, but was armed with a long knife. When he stood up the firelight struck it, sending its reflection back. Samuels knew the Apache were noted as the greatest knife fighters on earth. They were snake fast and full of tricks. If he was to get this one, he'd have to do it from behind and do it damn sudden.

Creeping slowly backward until he felt it was safe to stand, he crept up the slope and hearing the rattle of stones, peered into the darkness. Too late he sensed, rather than heard, the onrush of moccasined feet, then the Apache hit him low and hard in the kidneys and Samuels fell with a gasp. He lost his gun as the Apache fell with him and before he knew what was happening, he found himself with the Apache's deadly knife at his throat. He lay perfectly still and waited for death. It didn't come. Instead the Apache picked up his gun and pulled him to his feet. Looking around he discovered all five of the Indians standing around him. He was dragged to the fire and dumped unceremoniously on the ground, where he sat up and waited. With bitterness he realized what a fool he had been to attempt to slip up on and take out five Apaches. Hell, even a man like Al Siebert, the great Indian fighter, wouldn't have been that much of a damn fool.

Sitting there waiting for death he wondered what in hell possessed him to send Sergeant MacIntosh south. He should have kept him with him, for two guns were always better than one and the sergeant knew Indians.

As he sat and cursed his own stupidity, the Apaches went about their camp chores as if he didn't exist. One of them cut long, thin slices of meat from what was obviously a deer flank while another mixed corn batter with water, making a thin paste, which he then wrapped in large leaves and pushed into the coals. Seeing the water used thus, Samuels pointed to the canteen and said, "Water?"

One of the Indians glanced at him then casually kicked a canteen over to him and then ignored him while Samuels took several careful swallows, lowered it and thought, that was damned near worth dying for then remembered all the stories he had heard about what these desert nomads did to prisoners and suddenly felt cold all over.

When the food was ready, the same Indian who had given him the water handed him two pieces of meat and part of a corn cake and again ignored him. Wolfing it down, Samuels thought wryly, the condemned man received his last meal and wondered how many men facing death were allowed even what he was given.

Finished, he waited to see what they would do next. They did nothing. So, Samuels decided to go to sleep and, following the decision, stretched out and, pillowing his head on his arm, closed his eyes, only to be jarred back to reality when one of the Apaches said something to the others and rose and trotted off into the night.

He was gone for a good ten minutes, then Samuels heard a horse walking and when the animal's shoe struck a rock and clattered, he thought, must be a white man, knowing Indians seldom rode horses that were shod unless they had just stolen them.

Sitting up Samuels stared into the night as a dark-clad figure rode into the camp on a big blue roan and stepped down and came to the fire.

Staring at Samuels, the Magician said, "So, Captain, we meet again."

"Looks that way," Samuels agreed.

One of the Apaches spoke to Kale and the gambler

answered in perfect dialect and Samuels wondered where the hell the man had learned the language.

"Samuels, this here Apache has just suggested I leave you in their tender care," Kale said. "Seems they know where there's a handy anthill near here and they figure it would be a pleasant way to pass the day tomorrow to tie you down over it, spread a little sugar around your eyes and mouth and watch those big old red ants do what they're so good at . . . eating flesh by the pound."

Samuels stared at him. "My God, Kale, what kind of a white man would turn another over to Apaches?"

"You, if I recall, had four of these fellows with you when you hit the stage. If we had resisted they would have killed us if they could. Right?"

"I wouldn't have allowed them to torture you," Samuels declared. "Hell, I may be hard, but man, I ain't hard enough to sic an Apache on a white man."

While the white men talked, the Apaches sat around the fire and smoked and watched. They did not speak among themselves.

"Mister, you'd do anything you decided to do if it would further your aims," Kale said and, handing his reins to one of the Apaches, unsaddled the roan and carried his rigging around the fire and dropped it while the Indian led the animal away to stake him out in the sparse grass growing at the far end of the little canyon.

Looking at the Magician, Samuels wondered what kind of man he really was. Some said Kale came from a wealthy eastern family, a not unusual thing to occur out here, for many young men of good family had come west seeking their fortune. Some found only lonely graves. Others got rich. Most went home as broke as the day they arrived. A few established homesteads and dug in and stayed. They were the nucleus of the civilization that would follow. Samuels had heard from one source that

Kale was an English lord or French count, but no one knew for sure. It was known he was master of half a dozen languages, that he was a fine gambler whose luck often wound up getting him into gunfights because those who played against him just couldn't accept the fact a man could be that lucky. Kale was still around, which meant the challengers had played their last poker game.

Looking at him across the fire, Samuels wondered if he was as fast with the twin guns he wore as others said he was. The stories told around Tucson, Phoenix, Tombstone and other mining communities made him out to be as fast as Wild Bill Hickok had been, and as merciless as John Wesley Hardin or Bill Longley. There were even several bets going that the Magician could beat Leatherhand in a standup shootout.

Samuels had long ago decided that was one bet he didn't want either side of.

Now he said, "Mr. Kale, when I took that stage, I knew you worked for Marcus Bell," and was gratified to see that bothered Kale.

"I figured on making you an offer that would beat anything Bell might be paying . . ."

The Magician looked at Samuels for a long moment then said, "He's paying me $1,000 a month. Can you beat that?"

"Hell, yes," Samuels avowed. "We're ready to offer you $1,500."

Kale stood up and went to one of the Apaches and said something and the Indian dug coffee from Kale's saddle-bags and filling a smoke-blackened pot with water from a canteen, dumped in the Arbuckle and pushed it into the edge of the glowing coals.

Watching the process, Kale suddenly conjured up two cigars, seemingly out of thin air. Handing one to Samuels, he took a tiny pair of gold clippers from a vest pocket and nipped the end off his and tucked it into his mouth. When Samuels had followed suit, Kale reached out a casual finger and flame leaped from it to light both cigars.

The Indians, their eyes wide, talked in guttural voices of amazement. Then Kale turned and, holding up his hand in the firelight, made a quick motion and suddenly produced a long, thin dagger. Whipping it around in a circle, he flipped his wrist again and the blade vanished as if it had never been. Again the Indians muttered to each other.

"Them's pretty handy tricks," Samuels observed.

Kale smiled and said, "Here's one that's even handier," and thrust out his arm and suddenly there was a gun in his fist.

With a quick movement Kale made the gun disappear again.

"I never heard of a man using a .45 Colt for a sleeve gun," Samuels said.

Wordlessly, Kale held his arm out and Samuels felt all around it. There was no hideout harness.

"Where the hell did that thing come from?" he asked.

"Ever hear of the Nabb family?" Kale asked.

Samuels shook his head.

"They were Mormons. Involved in the Mormon wars out in Utah. They perfected a draw in which they merely stuck out their arm and a gun appeared in it and they fired. Needless to say, nobody ever beat them. They killed half a dozen men before folks left them strictly alone. It was kind of odd in a way, seeing as how they were really devout Mormons. Anyway, folks around Utah called their method the Nabb Draw. They died with the secret, but I figured out how they did it. I've used it ever since."

"Think you could beat this fellow Leatherhand with that rig?"

Kale smiled coldly. "That's exactly what I plan to do."

Samuels stared at him, then asked, "Any particular reason or you just wanta try his mettle?"

Kale gazed out into the dark Arizona night and said almost absently, "Let's just say the state ain't big enough to hold the both of us."

"You thought about my offer?" Samuels asked.

"I've accepted. If I hadn't of decided in your favor, you would already be on your way to the anthill," and Kale laughed a grating laugh that set Samuels's skin crawling.

Chapter III

Rebecca O'Brien sat naked in the big brass-bottomed tub and luxuriated in the hot water and the delicious smell of soap. This was her third bath since her arrival. She just couldn't seem to wash away the dirty feeling she had acquired while a captive of Samuels and his men. Finally, when the water began to cool, she rose and stepped carefully from the tub and stood drying herself with a large wool towel. As she did so, she glanced at herself in the mirror and liked what she saw there. She was pretty, her figure all curves and soft angles of enticement. Small and almost delicate-looking, she usually fooled people who overlooked an inner steel she possessed. Miss O'Brien could take care of herself quite adequately and she knew it. She also wasn't blind, which is to say that she knew exactly what her father, the senator, was up to. What she hadn't figured out yet was her role in all his machinations.

Thinking over her and the other passengers' kidnapping, she decided she had not been the target. She wasn't sure who was, but guessed that Samuels would probably have killed those he wasn't interested in and handed her over to his men to be used and then either killed or traded her to the Indians.

Then the mysterious Kale had escaped and someone

began shooting Samuels's men. She wondered if it was Kale, or that strange young man with the cold brown eyes who had suddenly appeared at the Riverside Stage Station. Now what did they call him, she asked herself, trying to bring his image back, but couldn't recall. Tossing the towel onto the floor, she walked to the wall and rapped on it sharply with her fist, then went to the door and waited. When the knob rattled, she stepped to one side and un- locked it and smiled as Wolf came in, closed and locked the door behind him and took her naked body in his arms.

Gazing up into his eyes, she said, "My goodness, hand- some stranger, where in the world did you come from?"

Vent Torrey and Arkie Chan rode northeast from Dragoon. They each carried four canteens, enough food for five days and gold-panning equipment. When they purchased the pans and rock picks at the Dragoon mercantile, the genial owner had said, "Boys, if you're planning on going into the Pinaleno Mountains, you best leave your names and the addresses of your next of kin. That there is Chiricahua Apache country."

"I thought they were the white man's friend now," Vent said.

"Shore they are," the storekeeper agreed, "that is, as long as the boys in blue at Fort Bowie are keeping an eye on them, but let 'em catch a couple of fellers like you out there where nobody knows what's going on and they'll murder and eat you for breakfast."

"Never knew they was cannibals," Chan said and they paid and left the storekeeper shaking his head.

As they crossed into the foothills of the Pinaleno Mountains, the going got rougher and rougher. Huge boul- ders lay strewn over the land as if hurled there by a playful giant. Rocky cliffs jutted upward several hundred feet, their sheer sides as smooth as an adobe wall. Jagged cuts in the land made traveling difficult, for each time the two men struck one, they were forced to ride around it, or seek a way down into the gut of the canyon and back out again.

Riding past a flat rock, Vent glanced at the rattler coiled there, his tail up and his rattles buzzing a warning, and said, "Don't fret, old feller, I ain't about to invade your territory," and rode on.

A huge tarantula squatted beneath an octillo and stared out at them, its furry body exuding curiosity. Vent knew their bite was not fatal, but he still didn't want to test it. He also knew that beneath every rock a centipede lurked, his tail curled and ready to strike, and that gila monsters came out in the early morning to bask in the sun, then vanished deep in some burrow, waiting for the coolness of night to hunt.

A coyote trotted away from them, stopping occasionally to look back, his eyes wise and full of sneak, then vanished as if swallowed up by the desert.

The horses were beginning to feel the heat now and Vent decided it was time for a rest. Riding into a palo verde grove, he stepped down, loosened the cinch and, dropping the reins, went to one of the canteens and filling his hat, allowed the Appaloosa to drink it, then took his own water ration from the mouth of the canteen.

Looking at Chan, who wore his dark gambler's clothes, but had removed his coat and carefully tied it behind the cantleboard, Vent observed, "You look like you're on your way to preach a sermon."

Chan grinned impassively and went and sat down on a rock. As he stared toward the mountains, he suddenly narrowed his eyes, stood up and walked to the edge of the grove and gazed eastward. A thin column of smoke was edging skyward and, as he watched, it suddenly broke up in a series of small clouds then resumed its original shape.

At the same time, Vent, who had gone to the other side

of the grove to check their back trail, saw smoke to the south of them.

"Looks like the Apaches know we're here," he said, and Chan nodded and pointed east.

Vent had his look then walked back and sat down. Chan also resumed his former position and digging out a cigar, lit it and watched Vent roll a cigarette and fire it up.

"How close?" Chan asked.

"Hard telling," Vent replied. "Could be 20 miles or twenty feet. Never know with Apaches."

"You fought them once, didn't you?"

Vent nodded. "Tangled with them half a dozen times in the north. They almost put Owney Sharp under once when we was in the Verde Valley."

Chan smiled. "A hard man to put down," he observed. Sharp had ridden with both men and Leatherhand considered him one of the all-time great gunfighters. He was one of those men who possessed perfect coordination. He was also a man known throughout the southwest as totally merciless, a factor in his personality that sometimes bothered Vent, although he knew in his heart that for a man with Sharp's enemies to keep on surviving he had better be merciless. The fact that Hitch Hawks was now in Arizona and would try and kill him on sight was a graphic example of what was wrong with Vent's philosophy. He had once let Hawks out from under his gun and that was a mistake he had since vowed he would never make again.

"Better move along," Chan said and Vent nodded and rose, cinched up the Appy and watched Chan mount the big black stud he had owned for several years and they moved out, still traveling northeast and ignoring the smoke signs.

Vent knew better than to try and run. To do so would be to set the Apaches on their trail like animals. No, they would continue on and if the Indians jumped them, they would handle it as best they could.

They were a good twenty miles into that wild country when they saw their first Apache. He appeared from a canyon half a mile to their right, rode out on a rocky knob and sat watching them. Vent immediately looked to the west and there was the Apache's counterpart on another knoll.

"Reckon they figure they got us boxed?" Chan asked conversationally.

"No, that ain't the idea," Vent said. "They're trying to shove us down into that canyon just ahead. You can bet they's half a dozen or so ambushed up there waiting for us. Hell, we'd never make her out of there."

"So, what now?"

Turning his horse, Vent rode directly toward the Indian on their right and Chan followed, watching to see what the Apache would do. He wasn't long in finding out. One moment the Indian was there and the next he had vanished.

Vent smiled and rode on, but he lifted his rifle free of the scabbard and jacked a shell into the chamber. Chan followed suit.

When they reached the knob where the Indian had been, he was nowhere in sight, but Vent knew the Apache lurked somewhere nearby. Riding carefully along the spur ridge that led away from the knob, he glanced west and noted the second Apache was pacing them.

When he looked back, the first Apache appeared suddenly fifty feet ahead of them. Vent continued to ride directly toward him. Again he was swallowed up by the desert and still the second Indian came on.

"Now they'll know their trap has been sprung and they'll come out of that canyon behind us," Vent said.

Chan glanced back and saw Vent was right. He counted

seven Indians riding wiry little desert ponies as they broke free of the canyon 200 yards behind them.

"Nine," he said.

"Can probably figure they's at least three or four more hid out as backups," Vent said.

Again Chan looked back and saw the seven braves were following them at a sedate pace, each holding a Spencer rifle butt down against his leg. Watching these desert nomads come on, Chan knew he was looking at some of the finest fighters in the world. They were trained to fight almost since birth, as their forefathers before them had been. And they were not like other tribes. They found no glory in risking their lives to count coup. That, they considered stupid. If they risked their lives, it was to leave a man dead behind them. An Apache took no chances. If he was outnumbered, he scattered to the desert winds and returned later when the scales were balanced in his favor. He lived off the land and had no qualms about eating his horse or some rancher's mule, a delicacy he delighted in. He would ride a horse until it dropped, cut it up and eat it, then continue on foot, covering fifty miles from sunup to sundown. They called themselves "The People" and to them all other humans were little better than animals. These were the men who followed them now and Chan wondered if he and Vent had run out their string.

Vent, seemingly unconcerned, continued riding along the ridgetop in almost arrogant disregard of the danger the Apaches posed. Then the Indian who had been appearing and disappearing in front of them suddenly popped up again and raised his rifle, aiming it at them.

Vent rode on.

Chan watched and waited, his rifle slightly canted forward, his eyes on the Apache.

The Indian vanished again. Chan glanced back and those to the rear had closed up the gap and were now about 100 yards behind them. Still they rode on until the ridge finally started to drop down toward a wide valley that butted up against the base of Pinaleno Mountain.

Turning his head, Vent said casually, "You better have six beans in each wheel because if they plan to hit us now's when they'll do it."

Chan grinned. "Old rule," he said. "Never put more than five shells in a Colt. Man could shoot himself if he keeps one under the hammer."

"Yeah, you're right . . . safety first," Vent said and grinned and then the Indian who had been popping up in front of them suddenly appeared, swung his rifle up and fired.

The slug screamed between them. Chan, looking back, saw it strike the dirt almost directly in line with the Apaches behind them, then whine away to lose itself in the desert.

Vent fired back instantly and his slug slammed the Apache sideways off his horse and into the brush. Vent gave his horse the gigs and whirled him off to the right and Chan jumped the stud down the bank to the left, wheeled him, lifted his rifle and fired five rapid shots and was rewarded when one of the trailing Apaches, coming on at a hard run with his rifle raised, suddenly somersaulted backwards off his horse and vanished among a stand of creosote brush.

As if his fall was a signal to the others, they dropped from sight and Vent called, "Off the horses or they'll skyline us," and dropped free from the Appy just as a bullet whipped through the space he had so recently occupied.

Chan hit the ground and jerked the stud down and Vent, whose Appy had been war-trained by the Ute, followed suit. Neither man wanted his horse shot dead.

Lying behind a rock, Vent watched the brush carefully.

Something moved and he fired and was rewarded by a high, gurgling scream.

Chan, having found his own rock five feet from Vent, suddenly rolled on his back and fired point blank at an Apache who had leaped from behind another rock and was running down on him with a huge knife in his fist. Chan's bullet took him square in the face, killing him instantly.

He had barely hit the ground when a second Indian rose from beneath a bush and fired almost point blank at Vent. Somehow the bullet missed and Vent, in the process of jacking a round into the rifle, knew he'd never make it before the Indian fired a second time, dropped the long gun and drew his .44 as fast as he had ever shucked it in his life and shot the Apache through the chest, knocking him backward, where he lay twitching in the throes of death.

Chan fired at something moving fifty feet in front of him and was startled when a javelina broke cover and squealing, ran down the slope. Then the sound of on-rushing horses' hooves jerked both men around. Three Apaches were riding toward them along the slope. They were bent far over their horses' shoulders, their rifles protruding from behind the animals' necks.

"Watch behind us," Vent shouted and stood up and fired once. His bullet struck the lead horse squarely in the forehead and the animal screamed and reared over backward, crashing into the other two and carrying all three down the slope together. Ignoring Chan, Vent ran to the edge of the drop and methodically picked off the Apaches as they floundered free of the fallen animals. Whirling, he was in time to kill one of two Indians that were firing at Chan. The half-breed brought the other down.

Suddenly the desert was silent again, disturbed only by the distant sounds of gun thunder echoing off the towering face of the Pinaleno Mountains.

When Chan would have risen, Vent shook his head. "Hold the position. If there's still one out there, he could nail us both."

So they waited for half an hour, then Vent crawled off toward where he had downed the first Apache. There was blood, but no Indian.

Instantly alert, he rose on all fours and gun up, carefully looked around. Nothing moved in all the broad expanse of that wild land but still Vent remained crouched, his ears attuned to the slightest sound. Finally, after a long five minutes, he was rewarded. The sound of shallow breathing came to him from a stand of chaparral. Lifting the rifle he aimed at the bushes and fired and fired again. A gasp and thrashing noises came from them, but still Vent waited. Then he saw a leg thrust into view, the foot twitching uncontrollably. Sighting on the leg, he fired again. The Apache screamed and suddenly lunged upright, leveled his rifle and Vent shot him through the head.

"This time I reckon he'll stay dead," he muttered and stood up and went to his horse and looking at Chan, observed, "These damn Apaches is as hard to kill as a rabid dog."

Mounted again, they carefully scouted out each body and made sure no life remained. One of the dead Indians had been carrying a silver-plated Sharps and Vent stepped down and retrieved it and noted the initials carved on the stock. Looking up at Chan, he said "Wonder who T.L. was?"

"Well, I got me a hunch that whoever he might have been, he ain't got no need for that thing now," Chan observed.

Vent tied the weapon behind his cantleboard and then checked out the rest of the Indians' rifles, discovering they were Spencers of inferior quality.

"Look like trade guns, don't they?" he said.

61

Examining one, Chan nodded. "Probably the reason they couldn't hit nothin' with them."

"Our luck," Vent observed and they rode toward the valley, leaving the Apaches where they fell.

Looking up at the sky Chan remarked, "Damn buzzards already in the air. They can smell death quicker than an undertaker."

Samuels sat on a handmade bench, his spurs hooked over a rail fronting the fifty-foot-long veranda that ran the full length of the adobe building he called his headquarters. It sat almost flush against the face of a towering cliff that thrust straight up from a 200-acre valley, effectively blocking the northern end of it to anything bigger than a lizard or hawk. On the west and east the valley was tightly enclosed by similar cliffs that lay in a wide arch, finally coming together at the south end to form a narrow pass barely wide enough for a horse and rider. Halfway along the deep narrow cut leading into the hidden valley, cliff dwellers from some long-dead past had built their houses in caves high on the cliff walls, partially hidden from view by overhanging bluffs from above and outthrust lips of rock from below. There were two of these strange relics, one on each side of the narrow gap in the cliff, and Samuels had discovered a tunnel leading from inside these caves down through solid rock and into the valley just inside the narrow entrance.

They were the perfect guard posts. No one could reach them from below unless he made it inside the valley and no one could reach the inside of the valley unless he could find a way past the guards.

Along each side of the valley, a line of rough adobes faced each other across a broad street. Behind each adobe was a small corral and halfway along the lone street a lake, covering five acres and fed by a spring, furnished cold, sweet water the year around. There was plenty of feed for the horses, and half a dozen stolen steers, in the lower part of the valley.

Above the headquarters adobe where Samuels now took his ease, a Confederate flag hung motionless in the windless air.

This was Leesville, an almost impregnable fort in the heart of Apache country. It was peopled by outlaws and refugees from northern law; men who had spent the war years looting and killing along the Kansas-Missouri border in the name of the "Cause." There were guerrillas, members of the now-disbanded Confederate Volunteers of Texas and just plain gunmen with a price on their heads and nowhere left to hide.

Halfway along the street a squat building housed a crude bar where a Mexican sold Indian whiskey and tequila to the population. The place had no doors and Samuels was fond of saying it didn't need them because it never closed.

There was only one rule controlling the conduct of the drinkers; if two men entered into a gunfight, the survivor was immediately hanged. In a fight occurred, it was settled with fists and as most gunmen had a distinct aversion to fighting with fists, there weren't many such duels.

Samuels backed up his regulations with six hardcases, all of them with reputations as mankillers. They never drank and they stayed away from the two dozen females that lived in the town. These women had been brought to Leesville by men, some of whom still lived there while others had moved on, following mysterious duties assigned them by Samuels. Some of the women, on the dodge themselves, had heard of Leesville and had a man bring them there. They earned their keep by being always available when a man needed a companion for the night, by cooking and washing and keeping the cabins clean.

Samuels ran the town as if it were a military post. Men

pulled regular guard duty and if they got drunk while doing it, they were shot. Since the town had been built three men had died at the end of a rope, then left dangling from a large oak tree growing near the lake. Two men had been shot for getting drunk on guard duty and a third publicly horsewhipped for dallying with a woman while doing guard duty.

Samuels had little doubt that the authorities knew about Leesville. It had not been his purpose to keep it a secret. On the contrary, he wanted them to know it was here. No army post in southern Arizona had the manpower to broach Leesville's defenses. Half a dozen good riflemen could easily hold it forever and take a dreadful toll of any enemy foolish enough to attempt to storm it.

From this sanctuary, Samuels planned to launch a series of stagecoach and bank robberies, raking in enough money to build a political machine that would eventually wield enough power to take over the state. Already there was one such machine, so Samuels had been told by Quade Garvey. It was headquartered in Phoenix and Prescott, but its tentacles held half a dozen major mining centers in their clutches. Tombstone was one of them. With its millions in silver being dragged from the earth, it was a plum worth plucking.

Sheriff Johnny Behan was the man given this task. Samuels knew his plans had gone awry when the Earp family killed off his muscle in a blazing gunbattle on that town's streets, then murdered half a dozen more before fleeing the state.

The way Samuels saw it there was now a power gap. He would use Senator Burgess . . . who thought he was using Samuels . . . and when he no longer needed him, he would arrange for his sudden demise. Quade Garvey was also a pawn in his game, as was Ah Kee, the contact with the gunrunning elements in Mexico. Samuels did not delude himself into thinking one load of guns would do the trick. He must equip an army and put it in the field. An army had to have weapons. Weapons cost money. Quade Garvey was the money man. Through his association with Ah Kee, he was able to line up the guns and the gold to pay for them. Samuels did not know what Ah Kee expected to get out of all this and he didn't care. The Chinaman wasn't that important as far as Samuels was concerned. There were a dozen men around with contacts south of the border. Ike Clanton, the survivor of the Earp-Clanton gunfight, was one. He had extensive contacts south of the border. Others were as well-connected.

Because of such contacts Samuels cared little for Ah Kee and would have him killed if it became necessary.

The plan wasn't foolproof. There was Vent Torrey. Two days ago Sheriff Phillip Rodriguez rode into the valley and passed on the information that the man called Leatherhand had met with a strange half-breed Chinese gambler in Dragoon and the two then rode north the same day. Thinking about Rodriguez, Samuels figured Garvey used his head when he bought the lawman. He would come in handy.

Now he had the Magician, that strange and mysterious trickster, in his camp and working for him. He felt fine. He couldn't lose. The chess pieces were all falling in place and all he had to do was play a careful game. The fiasco with the stage passengers would be his last error.

"Surveying your kingdom?" The Magician interrupted his reverie.

Glancing over his shoulder, he saw the tall, black-clad man had come to the porch and was now leaning against the wall, a coffee cup in his hand, gazing at Samuels quizzically.

"I was thinking of sending you out in search of this gent

65

Leatherhand. It makes me nervous, not knowing where he is,'' Samuels said.

"Don't worry about Leatherhand," Kale assured him. "He's my problem."

Sargeant MacIntosh came out and went to the rail and sat on it, a bottle in his hand and looking slightly flushed.

Staring at him, Samuels cautioned, "Go easy on that stuff, Mac. I need you sober."

"Just warmin' my blood up for a little visit down to Marie's cabin," MacIntosh replied and took another drink.

"That hellcat's gonna strip you of your manhood if you ain't careful," Samuels said.

Then the Magician walked to the far end of the veranda, turned casually and said distinctly, "Captain Samuels, the young lady you kidnapped on that stage was Senator Burgess's daughter. He's a little upset about it. In fact, he's so upset he sent me along to administer a lesson," and as Samuels, eyes wide with shock, half-rose, Kale conjured up a .45 and shot him through the chest, the bullet snapping dust from his shirt an inch to the left of his breast pocket. Spinning, he went off the steps and rolled down into the yard.

"Why, you yeller bastard!" MacIntosh screamed and went for his gun. He made a good try, but was woefully slow. Kale put his second bullet through the sergeant's head, kicking it back against a porch support, then he flopped over the rail and died with his arms and upper body hanging head down, a stream of blood waterfalling into the dirt below.

As men broke from the cantina and several adobes along the street, the Magician made the .45 disappear at the same moment two of his Apaches appeared from each end of the headquarters building and two more stepped around the corners of the two adobes at the north end of the street. They held 38.40 Winchesters in their hands and, when the running men stopped before the veranda and stared at the two dead men, Kale nodded amiably toward the Apaches and observed, "Yonder are four Apaches. They're armed with repeating rifles. Any man who touches a gun is dead."

A towering giant of a man wearing a Confederate forage cap and a cavalry sword at his hip pushed his way to the front of the mob and called out, "What the hell's going on here, Kale?"

"Just a little change of leadership," Kale said.

"Hell, Samuels was doin' all right," a little weasel of a man wearing two guns that looked heavy enough to use to weight him to the bottom of the lake, called out.

"He made some errors so I was sent along by the men who are actually responsible for Leesville to straighten them out," Kale said. "They have been handled. I'm in charge now. You boys take your orders from me."

The big man snorted. "What if we don't want to take orders from you?"

Kale looked at him, then suddenly conjured up a gun and shot him in the face. The bullet smacked into his skull, whipping his head back viciously and jerking him part way around. The man, dead on his feet, still remained upright as the crowd moved back, staring at him with consternation. Then, like a great tree, he slowly toppled over, smashing face down in the dirt of the yard, where he lay unmoving.

"Kilt him deader than a damned nit," the weasel-faced man observed, then looked up at Kale and said, "I reckon you made your point, Magician. Will things be the same as before?"

"Just the same," Kale assured him.

"Hell, then let's get back to our drinking," another man voted.

Nodding at the three dead men, Kale said, "Four of you fellers carry those things over to the south end of town and plant them. Reckon it's as good a time as any to start a boot hill.''

High on the bluff overlooking the valley, Vent turned to Chan and said, ''Now the Magician's running the show.''

Colonel Royce C. Bedlam had spent almost fifteen years on the fronter, most of it fighting Indians. Now he was being asked to attack and capture an American settlement. As he marched across the parade ground at Fort Bowie, he thought how typical it was of the Army to assign a man whose expertise lay with his knowledge of Indians and Indian fighting to a mission totally foreign to him. He wasn't enthusiastic about leading men into the Chiricahua Apache stronghold to capture some town being defended by a bunch of outlaws, killers and their pro-slaver masters.

Reaching the far side of the parade ground, he passed a sergeant with a woodcutting detail and, when the man saluted, almost missed it, then absentmindedly answered the salute and stepped up on the porch of the headquarters building and entered.

The corporal on desk duty stood up and assuming a position that reminded Bedlam of a wooden cutout in blue, snapped a salute and said, ''Sir?''

Bedlam answered the salute, ordered the soldier at ease and inquired, ''The general in?''

At that moment, General Crook stuck his head around the corner of his office door and said, ''Come in, Royce, come in.''

Crook, an unorthodox officer whose work with the Indians was being constantly circumvented by his own government, was that unusual man in uniform in the southwest who believed the Indians were actually human. He was known widely among the warring tribes and probably the only white man alive totally trusted by the Apaches.

Looking up sourly at Bedlam, he said, ''Sit down,

man,'' then growled, ''the government has done it to me again. They've ordered the Apaches back onto the San Carlos. Insane! I finally talked them into smoking the peace pipe and even got them to plant crops and start farming . . . farming! The Apaches, the most warlike tribe in America . . . and now those fools in Washington have ordered them off the land they've worked to plant. They even built a four-mile long canal . . . imagine that . . . a four-mile long canal built with worn-out equipment, broken tools and sheer muscle.''

Bedlam, who during his career had seen dozens of treaties broken, was no stranger to what Crook was now experiencing. Each time somebody in Washington decided to move the Indians because a land speculator friend wanted it done, he automatically condemned dozens of settlers to a terrible death, for the Apaches always reacted in the same way; they ran amuck, killing, raping, looting and burning.

Looking tiredly out the window, Crook asked, ''What can I do for you, Royce?''

''Men and equipment,'' Bedlam said.

''I suppose this has to do with Leesville?''

Bedlam nodded, knowing that with Crook's contacts he would have as much or more information than almost anyone else in Arizona, ''I suppose they've explained to you what my assignment is?''

Crook stood up and went to a window and gazed out toward the ragged mountains to the north and said, ''Yes, they've told me. These pro-slavers are still at it. Now I'm told they've set up their own little kingdom out in the Pinaleno Mountains.''

''You recall Captain Samuels?'' Bedlam asked.

Crook turned and looked at the colonel and said, ''Oh, yes, I remember him. Cashiered for cowardice, wasn't he?''

''Yes,'' Bedlam nodded. ''He was lucky he wasn't

shot. The only thing that saved him was family connections. Instead he was kicked out of the Army and given a civilian assignment in Washington for the duration of the war.''

''And now he's building an army of his own,'' Crook mused.

''Not his, General,'' Bedlam said and wondered if he should go into details, then decided he had no choice. ''Man named Marcus Bell, he's the anti-slaver that destroyed Freedom, Missouri, he's heading up one faction. The man behind the other is Senator Carl Burgess and his aide, Quade Garvey . . .''

Crook returned to his desk and sat down heavily. ''Now isn't that a mess? What an unsavory barrel of fish . . . And what a time for it to happen. The Apaches will start raiding as soon as the Army at San Carlos gets careless, and they will, mark me, they will.''

Bedlam wished he had a drink, but knew Crook was a teetotaler. ''What we've learned so far isn't very encouraging. A gun shipment is due at Leesville out of Mexico within the next ten days. Garvey is handling that. A man named Hitch Hawks, a Missourian, brought the guns across the border. I'm told there's a Gatling in the shipment.''

Crook turned and stared at him. ''A Gatling? Where the devil did they find that?''

''Damned if we've been able to discover, sir, but it's there. This fellow Hawks, he spent the war fighting with Bloody Bill Anderson and Quantrill and they say he's as hard as an anvil. Then there's another odd element in this . . . A man folks call Leatherhand has turned up and taken a hand in the game. Why, I don't know, except for the fact that he and his family have been feuding with the Hawks family for so long, they've each forgotten what the feud was all about. I first met Leatherhand, or Vent Torrey, his real name, while he and his mother and sister were crossing the great plains from Kansas to Colorado. Young

Vent, he was just a wet-eared boy then, had wound up the only survivor after a gunfight with the Hawks near Dodge City. He had a badly damaged hand and I turned him over to our surgeon, who had to tell him he'd never use the hand for anything again.

"Well, General, he fooled us all. He not only regained the use of it through some kind of odd leather contraption I'm told a Ute shaman in Colorado made for him, but he's now considered one of the fastest men with a handgun on the frontier. There are those who say that even Hickok couldn't beat him."

"A gunfighter," Crook said.

"Not just a gunfighter, sir. More than that. He's marshaled around the country and they say he sells his gun to no man. He's been in half a dozen range wars, but from what I hear he seems to fight on the right side. Now he's in southern Arizona and if it hadn't been for him, I would have gotten a firsthand look at Leesville."

Crook nodded. "I read your report. You think it was this Torrey who whittled down Samuels's men?"

"I'm absolutely certain," Bedlam said.

"Where's he at now?"

"He was last seen riding out of Dragoon with a half-breed Chinese gunman named Arkie Chan, a man almost as fast with a pistol as Torrey himself."

Crook stood up and walked to the window again. Then turning, he shook his head. "Too many variables in all this. Royce, you are going to have to tread carefully. We can't point a finger at Burgess or Garvey unless we catch them with the goods, as they say. But on the other hand, we've got to stop those guns from reaching Leesville."

"Unless Garvey turned them over to someone else to deliver, he's still with them," Bedlam pointed out.

"How can we use this Leatherhand?" Crook asked.

"I don't know if we can use him at all, sir. He's

71

damned independent, goes his own way and does things the way he wants. He's also got some tough friends.''

Crook thought a moment then asked, "Say, he isn't the man who broke the Denver combine, is he?''

Bedlam smiled. "Yes, he is.''

"Heck of a job, that," Crook acknowledged. "Why don't you try and find him and hire him as a civilian guide or scout or something?''

"All right, General, I'll try it . . . Now, I need twenty-five men and the equipment for a thirty-day campaign . . .''

Crook slid a piece of paper in front of him and taking a quill pen, scrawled the necessary orders across it and signed it with a flourish. "That should do it, Colonel. Now, I want you to keep your eyes open. See if you can pick up Indian sign out there. I'm going to send Nantaje with you. He's been with me since the battle of Salt River and one of my best Apache scouts.''

Bedlam left the general's office and made his way to the commissary, purchased half a dozen personal items, then walked to Officer's Row, where he hunted up Captain Duane Speers.

When Bedlam entered the officer's quarters, he found Speers sprawled on his cot sound asleep. Tapping him on the boot, he said quietly, "On your feet, Captain," and watched as Speers slowly opened his eyes.

Staring up at Bedlam he said softly, "Oh, oh. I knew this duty was too good to be true. When old Bedlam comes riding in, look out . . .''

Bedlam smiled. "Is that any way for a soldier to address his superior officer?''

"It is if you are trying to get court-martialed," Speers said, sitting up and fishing out a cigar, which he managed to get fired up after several attempts.

He was a lean whiplash of a man with intelligent blue eyes and a handsome face that had gotten him into more

than one amorous adventure. The women liked him and
Speers liked women. He was also one hell of a soldier,
Bedlam knew, being one of the few men on the frontier to
have won the Medal of Honor in the Indian wars. Bedlam
had first encountered him while commanding a troop at
Fort Abraham Lincoln in the Dakotas during a period in
which the boy general, George Custer, was stationed there.
Speers did not like Custer, considering him a showoff and
an egotist and the feeling was mutual, with Custer refer-
ring to Speers as "that damned rakehell that can't even be
trusted to walk through Suds Row."

However, Bedlam knew that Speers, like Custer, was a
topflight cavalry officer in spite of his penchant for the
ladies. Looking at him now, Bedlam said, "Captain Speers,
you have now, as of this moment, been assigned to me.
You will sally forth from this place and gather me twenty-
five picked, experienced Indian fighters who have at least
been in Arizona long enough to know the difference between an ocotillo and a joshua tree."

Speers stood up and saluted smartly and then observed,
"Probably should make certain the poor devils write a
final letter to their loved ones and make arrangements for
the disposal of their bodies, if they are ever retrieved."

Bedlam, a smile in his eyes, continued, "You will draw
thirty days rations for these men and make sure they are
mounted on the best the fort has to offer," and he handed
Speers Crook's scribbled orders and watched his face.

Reading them, Speers said, "Well, the old man's not
one to send a poor soldier to a certain death, so I guess
even if they are to be commanded by a madman, there's
some hope."

Suddenly serious, Bedlam said, "Duane, you make certain the men you choose are pro-north. I don't want any
southern sympathizers on this campaign . . . Understand?"

Staring into Bedlam's eyes for a long moment, Speers asked softly, "What the devil we going into, Royce?"

"I'm sorry, Duane, but I'm not at liberty to tell you at this time. Two days from the fort, I'll fill you in," and he turned and walked out, leaving a very puzzled Speers behind.

That afternoon Nantaje reported to Bedlam where he sat on the veranda of the quarters he had been assigned, his chair tilted back against the wall, his hat over his eyes.

The Indian came and squatted in the dust and looking up at Bedlam, said, "I am Nantaje . . . scout. I go with you."

Bedlam let his chair down and pushing his hat to the back of his head, looked at the Indian and saw an Apache of medium height, who wore knee-high moccasins, a worn pair of cavalry pants, a blouse with a sergeant's stripes sewn to the sleeves and a red rag tied around his head constraining long, black hair. Around his stomach he wore a wide shell belt filled with cartridges while he carried a Colt .45 Army in a flap holster on his right hip. On the opposite hip a Bowie knife in a leather scabbard dangled. A Winchester repeating rifle sat butt down in the dirt with the barrel leaning against his shoulder.

Looking at him Bedlam thought, now here's a tough-looking customer, and standing up came down and sat on the steps and looked into Nantaje's eyes and said, "You are famous among the men I have fought with."

Nantaje smiled. "You are great warrior . . . he, Crook, tell me . . ."

"Will you work for me?" Bedlam asked.

Nantaje pretended to think it over, then nodded. "I work for you."

"You know Captain Speers?"

Nantaje nodded.

"Go and tell him I sent you. He may need help."

Nantaje nodded again and rose and went away and Bedlam once again took up his former position in the chair.

Half an hour later as he dozed, he heard footsteps and opening his eyes found Rebecca O'Brien standing at the bottom of the steps gazing up at him. Leaning against the veranda was the man called Wolf, whose crooked grin was still in place.

Rising and removing his hat, Bedlam bowed and invited, "Miss O'Brien, won't you and Mr. Wolf join me," and waited until they had mounted the steps and found chairs then said, "If you'll excuse me a moment, I'll find an orderly and see if I can't rustle up something cool from the icehouse."

When he returned with a blond-haired private he said, "You have a grand choice, Miss O'Brien. You may have iced tea or iced coffee."

"Tea will be fine," she said in her slightly husky voice.

"I prefer ordinary coffee," Wolf said.

The orderly went away and Bedlam looked at his guests and finally asked, "What brings you two here? I was under the impression you were on your way to Bisbee, Miss O'Brien."

"As a matter of fact I was, but then I heard the Apaches had been ordered back to the San Carlos so I asked Mr. Wolf to guide me here. They say Geronimo may go on the warpath. I think I feel just a bit safer at the fort."

"And you probably are. Anyway, let me welcome you and hope your stay will be a pleasant one," Bedlam said, adding, "unfortunately, I have been ordered into the field and will be gone for several weeks."

Smiling, Miss O'Brien said, "Why, that's a shame. I was looking forward to some pleasant hours of conversation."

"Perhaps when I return," Bedlam said.

Then the drinks arrived and Bedlam took the opportunity to closely examine his guests. There seemed to be an easy familiarity between the two, almost as if they were man and wife. Bedlam, who had been married almost twenty years, and whose wife was now waiting for him to send for her, could recognize the undefined intimacy that seemed to exist between some people who were very close emotionally, and wondered. He knew very little about Wolf, except for the stories that described him as a very dangerous man with a gun. He had roamed the frontier states for several years and was known as a friend of such notables as Luke Short, King Fisher, Ben Thompson and the Mastersons, Ed and Bat. No one seemed to know where he came from and few even knew what he did to earn a living. Some said he gambled and was marvelously lucky at it. Others claimed he was a hired assassin who charged highly for his services. Yet others claimed they had been told his family was wealthy and that they paid their black sheep son to remain in the west where he was safely out of the way.

"Mr. Wolf, what are your plans now?" Bedlam asked.

"Haven't really decided yet," Wolf said noncommittally.

"The Army's hiring teamsters, horsebreakers and scouts, if your interest lies along any of those lines," Bedlam informed him.

Wolf glanced at Miss O'Brien and then said, "Well, I've kinda promised Miss O'Brien's father I'd look out for her until she gets settled in Bisbee. Reckon I'll hang around here for awhile, unless the general's pulled in the welcome sign."

Bedlam shook his head. "I hardly think so. If you like, I'll have a word with him; explain to him that you are Miss O'Brien's protector while she's here in Arizona and that you'd like to remain at the fort for a while. I'm sure he'll be delighted to have you."

Wolf glanced at the girl and then looking at Bedlam, observed, "Sir, that's uncommonly kind of you."

Bedlam shrugged. "After all, Mr. Wolf, we were captives together."

"Have you heard the latest?" Miss O'Brien asked.

"I'm afraid I've been so tied up in army business I've lost touch," the colonel admitted ruefully.

"Samuels and that man he called sergeant have vanished. No one seems to know what happened. Mr. Wolf says he thinks the Apaches murdered them, but Captain Samuels seemed to get along quite well with them, seeing as how he had four traveling with him."

Bedlam smiled. "That's not how it works out here, Miss O'Brien. Some Apaches work for white men, some work for the Army and others are involved with such renegades as Samuels. They do what pleases them and no man really knows why they choose the way they do. We have several scouts here at Fort Bowie. They are faithful to a fault and their loyalty is unquestioned. Yet some of their kinfolks are raiding and killing whites."

Wolf nodded. "The Apache is a feller who believes in being his own man," he said.

Glancing up, Bedlam saw Crook approaching across the parade ground and rising, said, "Yonder comes the general. I'll introduce you."

He did not miss the look that passed between the girl and her gun-hung escort.

Chapter IV

Vent rolled from his blanket at first light and went about the careful preparation of the morning's breakfast fire. He selected the kind of wood that did not throw off smoke and kept the blaze small. They were camped in a valley a mile from the edge of the cliff overlooking Leesville.

They had been lucky. While circling the cliff tops above the town, the horses smelled water. Given their head, they turned west for a mile and carried Vent and Chan to this tiny valley where a spring seeped from the ground at the base of a cliff to form a small lake in a natural rock basin. Vent had been told there were many such water sources in the desert, but few white men knew their locations and the Apaches kept the secret of their whereabouts a closely guarded thing. It was their lifeline while traveling from one mountain range to another.

Al Siebert, the famous Indian fighter, once told Vent that if a white man knew where all the secret drinking spots were, he could travel across the desert anywhere and never fear running out of water.

"There's more water out there than white men realize," he said.

Vent had followed animal tracks and discovered such springs, but they were few and far between.

Chan sat up and threw off his blankets. First he donned his hat, then he stood up and strapped on his guns and then sat back down and pulled on his boots. That done, he rose and walked off into a stand of palo verde and relieved himself, then went to the spring and, still leaving his hat on, doused his face in the cold water, drank several handfuls and returned to the fire to find the coffee bubbling. Pouring a cup, he stood and drank it.

Vent had gone off to take care of the horses and now he led them to the rock bowl and allowed them to drink their fill. Leading the animals away again, he turned the Appaloosa free, but staked the black stud out to a palo verde.

Walking back to the fire, he poured himself a cup of coffee and stood drinking it as he said, "I think I'll hold off on the grain until we really need it. Them hosses are as fat as porcupine and about as sassy."

"The good life," Chan observed, then carefully set his coffee cup on a nearby rock and suddenly whipped his arm around and Vent saw a blur pass through the air so fast his eye almost missed it and a rabbit that had made the mistake of getting curious lay on its side feebly kicking.

Walking to the body, Chan bent and removed a star-shaped piece of metal about three inches in diameter from the animal's neck and returned carrying his prize.

"Breakfast," he said.

"What the hell is that thing?" Vent asked, staring at it.

Chan smiled. "It's called a *shuriken*. Dates to antiquity, so my Chinese relatives claim. A very efficient killer . . ."

"Isn't that the thing you put that gunny in California down with?"

Chan nodded. "It kills as fast as a knife and with practice anybody can beat a draw with it."

Handing it to Vent, he said, "Here, try it."

After Chan demonstrated the proper method of holding

79

and throwing it, Vent chose a barrel cactus as a target and hurled the *shuriken*, missing it cleanly.

Chuckling, Chan again demonstrated the strange weapon's use and this time Vent, who had a natural gunman's eye, sunk the deadly little star to the hilt in the cactus.

So they fell into a routine. Vent spent two hours a day practicing with both the *shuriken* and a slim-bladed dagger he had bought while in Tombstone. The rest of the day was spent spying on Leesville from the top of the bluff and exploring the area around the hidden outlaw town.

Most of it was desert, but the two gunfighters discovered several areas where the grass was green, denoting an underground water supply of major proportions, and on the west side of the valley they stumbled upon a cliff dwelling huddled inside a cave on the face of a sandstone cliff. While exploring it, they discovered yet another water supply.

The ancient rooms of the cave held dried food, utensils and weapons—apparently abandoned when the people who lived there left. Deep in the back of the cave, one room had been set aside for the dead and it was heaped with bones and skulls, many of them still with human flesh adhering to them.

Gazing at them Chan observed, "The desert is a great preserver of things," and Vent had to agree.

With each day's practice, Vent improved both his accuracy and speed with the dagger and the *shuriken*. When he finally reached a level of expertise matching that of Chan's, the half-breed dug out several stars from his saddlebags, each with a different dimension, and Vent started all over again. However, it didn't take him long to master these and finally, Chan, who had been watching his friend closely, nodded his satisfaction and presented him with three of the deadly instruments. Each was a different size. Then Chan showed Vent where to hide them in his clothes and how to get them into action and Vent spent several hours working on putting them into play. He kept the knife in its holster dangling down inside his shirt at the back of his neck and practiced with it from that position.

Watching him on their sixth day in the little valley, Chan nodded his satisfaction. "You're damned good with both those things," he said. "Almost as fast as you are with a gun."

Vent grinned. "I think I'm probably faster with the shuriken than I am with my forty-four."

Chan had to agree, but then reminded him, "You've got five chances in the wheel of your pistol and only one with the *shuriken*."

Thinking about it, Vent said, "I see the *shuriken* and the knife as edge weapons. The fact that a feller usually watches your gun hand gives a man an automatic extra second to nail him with the others."

"The element of surprise," Chan said.

Quade Garvey rode at the head of the column of pack mules. Behind him a dozen men, all armed with Winchesters, rode the flanks, their eyes restlessly wandering from rock to rock and canyon to canyon in search of Indians or cavalry, for Garvey was no fool. He knew the desert telegraph would have warned General Crook by now that guns were on their way to Leesville. Garvey's only edge was the fact that he had a long lead on any troops. He did not fear Indians. Apaches were in no shape to attack at this time in large numbers and they were not noted for doing so anyway. They preferred to hit small outfits with five or six raiders, kill the men, run off with their stock and steal their weapons.

A white-haired rider wearing a black hat and black calfskin vest, and sitting a sweat-stained claybank horse, angled up alongside Garvey, nodded and said, "How far are we from this Leesville?"

"Near as I can figure, we're about two to three days travel," Garvey told him.

The man gazed off at the barren desert country they were passing through and observed, "This here piece of country ain't fit for man nor beast."

Garvey shrugged. "Hell, Gene, the Apaches thrive on it," and he looked around at the white-haired rider and grinned.

Gene Buelah had worked for Garvey for three years and Garvey still didn't know the man. He kept his own council and did his job. He didn't seem to be afflicted with the habits that plagued most men in this country, such as gambling, women or booze. He would take a drink, play a little poker and bed a dancehall girl, but he wasn't obsessed with any of it. Garvey knew him for a careful man. He wore four guns and when horseback, kept a rifle in one scabbard and a shotgun in another. Garvey once asked him about this and he shrugged and said, "Needed something to balance the horse."

Looking at him now, Garvey noted the crossed shellbelts with their Colt .44s, tied-down holsters and the twins to them in Wes Hardin shoulder rigs. Vent wondered if Buelah ever got confused on which gun to go for in an emergency. The fact that he had downed several men attested to his proficiency with them.

That night they made camp in a broad valley surrounded by low hills and, once the mules were unloaded, watered and staked out in a small patch of greenery beneath an ironwood grove and, the Gatling broken out and mounted on its tripod, Garvey sat down with Buelah and the two pored over a map.

"Looks like we gotta swing around that damn big pile of rock just north of here," Quade observed, placing his finger on a spot on the map.

Buelah slowly traced the trail marked in red, following

it northeast with a finger until it passed into the jumble of the Pinaleno Mountains and wound through a number of deep canyons, finally ending at a spot marked by a large X on the map.

"Two days," he said.

Garvey shook his head. "More like three, Gene. That's damn rough country up there."

"We gonna have enough water?"

Pointing at the map, Garvey said, "Right here is half a dozen rock bowls. They're filled with water year 'round. Comes from underground springs. It ain't the best water; got a little alkali in it, but not enough to hurt the stock."

Early the next morning a rider from Leesville showed up and was escorted at gunpoint to where Garvey sat eating a crude breakfast of meat and potatoes and harsh black coffee.

"Who ya got there, boys?" he asked, looking at the visitor, who was dressed in a ragged pair of Levis, a worn chambray shirt and hat that looked like it had weathered far too many hailstorms. He had been relieved of three guns.

One of Garvey's men jerked a thumb at the newcomer and said, "This here gent says his name's Ambrose . . . Titus Ambrose, from Leesville."

Looking at the man over his coffee cup, Garvey asked curiously, "Now just how did you happen to find us, Mr. Ambrose?"

"I had a map," Ambrose said, apprently not liking his reception.

"A map, huh?"

"I got a message for you . . . Delta Kale now runs Leesville. He up and kilt Captain Samuels and MacIntosh. Shot 'em deadern a side of bacon."

Gene Buelah had walked up in time to hear Ambrose's statement and now he looked at Garvey and observed,

"Old Samuels never did strike me as a man who had to work hard to be called downright stupid."

Glancing at the men who held Ambrose under their guns, Garvey said, "That's all right, boys. Just leave Mr. Ambrose to me. Give him back his hardware."

With his guns back in their holsters, Ambrose helped himself to the coffee and a plate of food and squatted by the fire, ignoring Garvey and Buelah.

Looking at him distastefully as he pushed food into his mouth, Garvey asked softly, "How long did it take you to reach us, Mr. Ambrose?"

"Three days," Ambrose said around a mouthful of meat and biscuit.

"See any blue bellies or Indians?"

Ambrose shook his head, his mouth too full to allow conversation.

Glancing at Buelah, Garvey said, "This feller's got the manners of a damned hog," and Ambrose stopped eating abruptly and looked up, his face suddenly red.

"Want me to choke him off?" Buelah asked conversationally, eyeing his intended victim coldly.

Staring around, Ambrose suddenly realized he wasn't out of the woods yet. Rising, plate still in hand, he said, "Hell, Mr. Garvey, I'm sorry as can be. Me, I ain't et for two days. I reckon I'm plumb starved."

Garvey shook his head, then asked, "How do you happen to know my name?"

"Why, the Magician, he described you to me. Said I wasn't to talk to anybody else. Give me a note, he did," and he dug out a soiled piece of paper and handed it to Garvey and went back to his plate while Garvey read the note then handed it to Buelah and asked, "You read this note, Mr. Ambrose?"

Ambrose looked ashamed, but admitted, "No, I can't read, Mr. Garvey."

Garvey glanced at Buelah and nodded and Buelah drew without hesitation and shot Ambrose through the body.

The bullet turned him partially around and when he swung back, he had a gun in his hand and screamed, "Damn you dirty rawhiders," and fired at Buelah and missed, sending his slug into a mule standing fifty feet from the fire. The animal grunted, then ran squealing along the valley until it finally ran head on into a big boulder and collapsed with blood pouring from its wound.

Buelah fired again, knocking Ambrose, to his knees, then as the doomed man slowly raised his gun, shot yet again, this time sending a slug through the messenger's heart. He went over backwards and Garvey watched coldly as the dying man slowly drew his knees up to his chest, then straightened them out with a violent kick and relaxed into death.

Staring at him, Buelah said, "Damned fool sure as hell took some killin'."

Garvey picked up the note where Buelah had dropped it. Glancing at it he observed, "First time I ever saw a man deliver his own death warrant."

One of the men who had brought Ambrose into camp and who had witnessed the man's killing, asked curiously, "What the hell did that note say?"

Garvey looked down at it and then up at the questioner and said, "It informed me that the bearer was a thief and a liar and no longer needed at Leesville and asked if I would please eliminate him once he had completed his report."

Colonel Bedlam, riding at the head of his column, suddenly raised his hand, halting the long line of troopers strung out along the canyon floor behind him and sat very still. The sound of gunshots had come clearly across the desert. Turning to Captain Speers, Bedlam said, "I make it four shots . . ."

Speers nodded. "That's what I counted."

"Captain, get Nantaje up here," and then rode to a large boulder and stepped down while waiting for the scout.

When Speers returned with Nantaje, the Indian slid off his horse and came and squatted on his haunches and looked at Bedlam wordlessly.

"Four shots to the north," Bedlam said. "You hear them?"

"Nantaje heard," the scout said.

"We will wait here. You ride up there and check it out. If you run into trouble, fire three fast shots," and he watched as the Indian mounted and rode forward. "Captain Speers, give the men the rest order but inform them the smoking lamp is not lit."

Nodding, Speers rode to where Sergeant Beech King sat his horse and said, "Sergeant, give the men permission to dismount, but tell them to keep alert . . . and no smoking."

King, a huge Negro who had been in the 7th Cavalry ever since he fled the south and slavery ten years earlier, grinned and rode back along the column. As he passed he spoke quietly to the men and they dismounted, but left their cinches tight and kept their eyes on the sides of the canyon. There was not one among them who had not tangled at least once with the Apaches and all had considerable combat experience. Speers had chosen well, Bedlam knew, and he was satisfied with his command. Looking back now he watched the mule skinners lead their animals beneath an overhanging rock out of the sun and out of the way in case of a sudden attack which, if it included the mules, could leave them short of water and rations.

Speers rejoined Bedlam and the two men waited for almost an hour, then King rode up and said, "Three men

coming from the north, sir," and the two officers stood
and walked to their horses' heads and waited.

Nantaje was in the lead. Following him were two men
and Bedlam smiled when he recognized Vent Torrey and
the half-breed, Arkie Chan.

When they rode up and stopped, Nantaje jerked his head
over his shoulder and said, "Leatherhand," and then he
dismounted and, squatting, unsheathed his Bowie and
scratched a crude map in the dust and looking at the
colonel, told him, "North. Big pack train. A talking gun.
Many men."

Glancing at Vent, Bedlam asked, "You see them?"

Vent nodded. "Them mules are loaded with boxes of
rifles and the 'talking gun' your scout mentioned is a brand
new Gatling. They got it all set up."

Turning to King, Bedlam said, "Sergeant, return to
your men and see that they stay on the alert," and King
touched his hat and rode along the column. Waiting until
he was out of earshot, Bedlam then said, "Rest your
saddles, gentlemen. We've got some smoke to make,"
and, when Vent and Chan had stepped down, looked at
Speers and said, "You know anything about Leesville,
Mr. Torrey?"

Vent picked up a stick and scratched a mark in the dust,
then nodded, but did not elaborate.

Bedlam removed his pipe and began absentmindedly
filling it. Speers glanced back at the men then said quietly,
"Sir, you ordered the men not to smoke," and Bedlam
stared at him for a moment then said, "You're right,
Captain. Thank you," and put the pipe away.

Looking at Vent, he said, "General Crook has author-
ized me to ask you if you would work for us . . ."

"In what capacity?" Vent asked.

"As a scout or a consultant on the Indians or whatever
the hell suits you," Bedlam replied. "You wouldn't neces-

sarily have to hang around us. You could roam around out there; keep an eye on Garvey, on Leesville . . .''

''You figure that's Garvey up ahead?'' Vent asked.

Bedlam nodded. ''It's him, all right. He took delivery of those weapons from Hitch Hawks over southwest of Tombstone, so our sources tell us.''

''Did they tell you who engineered the sale?'' Vent asked and glanced at Chan, who looked back impassively.

''As a matter of fact, they did. Man named Ah Kee. He set up the deal and arranged payment and delivery.''

Vent thought about that then asked, ''Any idea why?''

''Guess he likes money,'' Bedlam observed and Chan smiled faintly.

Nantaje cleared his throat. ''Shots fired by white-haired man. He killed other feller. Shoot 'em dead.''

Bedlam stared at him, then asked, ''Any idea why?''

Nantaje shook his head. ''Him just kill. Man lay dead at fire. Packer fellers ready to leave when I see.''

Vent looked at Bedlam and asked, ''You know this white-haired man?''

The colonel shook his head.

''I know him,'' Speers volunteered. ''He's a southerner from down in Tennessee somewhere. Fought all through the war. Won a couple of field decorations and was breveted in the field. Name's Eugene Buelah. Now he's a gunfighter and from what I hear, a pretty fair one.''

Vent looked at Chan and asked, ''You ever hear of this gent?''

Chan nodded. ''After the war he came to Texas. Did some cattle rustling to sort of make ends meet. Graduated into horses, and Texans, being what they are, got kind of down on him. They came looking for him with a rope so he left there at a high lope. Wound up at Cripple Creek. I played poker with him there.''

''He a gunfighter?'' Vent asked.

"He thinks he is," Chan said.

Vent looked at Nantaje and asked, "How far away you figure that pack train is by now?"

The Indian thought a moment, then said, "Two, maybe three mile."

Looking at Bedlam, Vent said, "You can light that pipe now," and Bedlam nodded at Speers. The captain rose and waved his arm at King and when the big sergeant pulled his horse in at the head of the column, told him, "Smoking lamps lit, but keep the men alert and ready to ride."

"Yes, sir," King said, and touched his hat and rode back to the troop.

Looking at Vent keenly, Bedlam asked, "You gonna accept my offer?"

Turning to Chan, Vent raised an eyebrow and waited until the half-breed nodded curtly, then turned back to Bedlam and said, "We're a package. You take me, you take Arkie too."

"With pleasure," Bedlam replied. "If just half of what I've heard about Mr. Chan's abilities is accurate, he will prove invaluable."

Vent smiled faintly and observed, "That's what happens when a man gets a reputation for knowing how to die standing up."

"Well, let's hope neither one of you are called on to prove that out," Bedlam said. "Now, how about filling me in on Leesville?"

Vent described the place and as he talked, Bedlam looked more and more sour. Finally, when Vent finished, he said, "Sounds like the perfect hideout. With that Gatling, they can defend the place forever."

Vent shook his head. "They gotta have targets for that gun. If there's nothing to shoot at, it's only a hunk of metal."

Bedlam stared at him. "If we go charging in there, they'll have twenty-five men to shoot at."

Vent grinned, then looked at Speers and observed, "Now ain't that just like the Army; charge straight in and get the hell shot out of them?"

Speers looked away when Bedlam leveled a sharp glance at him, then the colonel asked, "How would you deal with Leesville, Vent?"

"I'd lay up on the cliff top and, every time a man showed, day or night, I'd pick him off. I'd block that canyon so none of them can get out and they're caught in their own trap."

"You mean just open up on them?" Bedlam asked.

"Oh, you can call down for them to surrender first, if it'll ease your conscience, but they're gonna tell you to go suck roots," Vent said.

Chan, who had been listening, asked, "Colonel, you have any dynamite with you?"

Bedlam shook his head. "Too hot for it. Out here the damn stuff starts beading up and pretty soon you're carrying TNT."

Vent, liking Chan's idea, said, "Maybe we can just make our own bombs outa gunpowder."

"We've got a barrel of gunpowder," Speers nodded. "It's wrapped in wet sacking and packed in sawdust."

Vent looked at Arkie and asked, "How about firing the buildings? Think we can do it?"

Chan turned to Nantaje and asked, "How hard would it be for you to make a bow and some arrows?"

Nantaje smiled. "Pretty goddamn quick, I think."

Bedlam looked curious. "What's in that head of yours now, Mr. Torrey?"

"Nantaje makes a bow and some arrows. We wrap the ends of the arrows with gunpowder, rig a fuse, and fire them into the roofs of those buildings and they'll go up with a bang."

Bedlam, beginning to see the possibilities, said aloud. "But first we watch these boys and see what building they store the Gatling ammo in. Hell, maybe we'll get lucky and they'll put the gun inside."

Vent rose and said, "There's a way around the valley. We camped in a meadow east of the cliff face. Plenty of water there if we nurse it. From there we'll be looking right down their throats."

Bedlam thought about it then told Speers, "You take nine men and Nantaje and follow that column. As soon as they get inside the valley, bottle it up. Nothing's to get out of there, not even a damn bird."

Speers nodded, touched his hat and quickly mounted and rode back along the column, carefully tolling off men until he had his squad. Leading them back to where Vent and Bedlam sat, he said, "I'll use Nantaje to make liaison with you, Colonel, as soon as we're in position."

Looking at the Apache, Bedlam said, "Nantaje, you go with the captain. He'll tell you what to do," and he looked up at Speers and said, "Make damn sure they don't spot you. Keep in mind they will probably have a rear guard out. Better have Nantaje do the close scouting. If they spot him, they'll probably figure he's just a curious Indian, or maybe part of a small war party or hunting party. There'll be no reason to connect him with us," then he looked at Nantaje again and said, "If they pull you in, my friend, you're not to tell them anything . . . Understood?"

Nantaje nodded. "Damned outlaws get nothing from Nantaje," and he went and mounted his desert pony and led Speers's squad away through the jungle of saguaro and agave.

Vent brought Bedlam's troop into the valley above Leesville three days later and there they bivouaced, ignoring the fact that the Leesville outlaws might see their smoke fires.

Said Vent, "Let 'em know we're here. They ain't going anywhere," and Bedlam settled down to await contact with Nantaje.

He didn't have long to wait. Camp had barely been set up when the Indian rode past the guards and went directly to Bedlam, where he stopped in front of the headquarters tent, dismounted and squatting in the dust, said, "Captain, he ready. Say he hold pass for a hundred suns."

Bedlam smiled and nodded. "Get yourself something to eat, Nantaje, then head back and rejoin the captain. Tell him to remain exactly where he's at until further orders. Also inform him that he's to send you to me once a day in case I need to message him. Understand?"

"Goddamn betcha, Nantaje unnerstan'," the Apache said and rose and led his horse to the spring and watered him.

Vent, who had set up a small camp with Arkie Chan near the spring, walked over and nodding at Bedlam, asked, "Speers make her all right?"

"He's in place. I'm going to follow your plan, Vent. I'm going to go to the cliff and give the Magician a chance to surrender. If he refuses, then he and his men are fair game."

Vent nodded. "Like shooting ducks in a pond," he said and rose and waved to Chan, who came over leading the horses.

The three men, accompanied by a six-man squad, rode to the cliff where Bedlam stepped off his mount, walked to the edge and stared over. Two hundred feet below his boot toes, the crude outlaw settlement lay sprawled in the green jewel of the hidden valley.

Cupping his hands, Bedlam shouted, "You down there!" and was rewarded when the Magician, easily recognizable in his black garb, strode from the building with the Confederate flag attached to a pole above it, and looked up.

Several men followed him into the street while men and women left buildings all along the line of adobes and stood looking up at the tall figure in blue.

"This is Colonel Bedlam, Mr. Kale," the colonel shouted. "I want you and your men to lay down your arms and march out of that valley single file and afoot."

The Magician leaned against a hitching post and shouted back, "Why don't you come down here and get us? I guarantee we'd hand you a warm reception," and then Vent saw two men wheel the Gatling from beneath a shed just to the north of the saloon and swing its barrel around and begin cranking it upward to cover the cliff face. Walking to his horse, he pulled the rifle from its scabbard and returned and lying down, nuzzled it against his shoulder, took careful aim, and looked up at the colonel.

"If he refuses again, Mr. Torrey, bring down those men on that gun," Bedlam ordered.

"With pleasure, Colonel," Vent said as Bedlam raised his cupped hands and shouted again, "Last chance, Mr. Kale. Give it up now or suffer the consequences."

Kale turned his head and spoke to Garvey, who was standing on the veranda, then looked back at the cliff top and shouted, "Your deal, Colonel."

Glancing down at Vent, the colonel said quietly, "Now, Mr. Torrey," and Vent fired and fired again and watched clinically as the two men manning the Gatling suddenly spun away and fell heavily.

As the echoes of the shots died away, the Magician leaped up the steps and shoved Garvey inside the building as Gene Buelah whipped up a rifle and triggered several rapid shots.

With bullets ricocheting off the face of the cliff, Bedlam ducked back, but Vent remained where he was, knowing it's a lot harder to hit a target above you than one below you. Carefully he sighted on the white-haired Buelah and let drive and saw the rifle suddenly knocked spinning from his hand and cursed softly to himself as the man leaped back through the door to safety.

At the first shots, the population of Leesville suddenly vacated the main street, leaving the town looking like a ghost. Bedlam crawled back to the cliff edge, ordering his men to take up positions along the edge and to shoot anything that moved down there. Chan had mounted his horse and rode down canyon until he was in position to command the front door of the saloon, then dismounted and, taking his rifle, stood on the cliff edge and poured nine rapid shots through the door. All was quiet for a long breath, then a man staggered out of the place, turned half around and collapsed onto his back. He did not move.

On Bedlam's command, the six-man squad poured a murderous fire into the buildings and as Vent watched, he saw shakes blown from the roofs, pans hanging by the doors hole-punched and sent spinning and window shutters blasted to kindling. No one answered the vicious fire and finally Bedlam called a halt.

Moving back from the cliff, he stood up and told the corporal in charge of the squad, "Corporal Radowski, you and your men remain here. If anyone, man or woman, leaves those buildings, you shoot to kill. Is that understood?"

The corporal nodded, touched his hat and went back to his men as Bedlam mounted and accompanied by Vent and Chan, rode back to camp.

As the afternoon wore on, an occasional shot came to them from the cliff and once they heard what sounded like two flat reports from the entrance to the valley where Speers and his men stood guard.

*   *   *

While Colonel Bedlam sat on the cork that held the Magician and his master, Quade Garvey, tightly bottled in the Pinaleno Mountains, Hitch Hawks sat in a tavern in the small town of Cochise and drank whiskey and waited for the Chinaman, Ah Kee, to appear. He did not like doing business with a foreigner, particularly a Chinese. He had little trouble reading most men, but the impassivity of the Chinese race bothered him. They did not seem to become involved in violence very often, and when they did, it was never controlled violence.

"Another drink?" the owner of the Cochise Hotel asked.

Hawks glanced at him where he sat on the bar top with a bottle between his knees and said, "Bring a bottle," and watched the man roll off the backside of the plank and come up with a jug of indeterminate color. He tramped around the bar, running into its corner as he passed and almost dropping the jug, then reached Hawks's table and set it down with a bang. Hawks looked up at him for a long moment, then said softly, "I don't like men who guzzle their own damn poison. Get ta' hell away from me."

Too drunk to read the danger signs, the bartender pulled himself up to his full height and glaring at Hawks, said, "That'll be two dollars, sir."

Hawks's boot suddenly came up and slammed into the man's crotch and as he bent double with a moaning gasp, the old man drew his stag-horned .45 and slammed it viciously down on top of the drunk's skull. He fell sideways, landing face down in the sawdust and did not move.

An Indian woman, who had been standing at a kitchen door, came out and grasping the unconscious man by the bootheels, slowly dragged him from the room. As he bumped from view, a tall man wearing a badge stepped through the archway leading to the check-in desk and, walking around the bar, poured himself a drink, then, leaning elbows down on the plank, said, "Nasty habit . . . beating up drunks."

Hawks, who still held the .45 in his hand, looked narrowly at the lawman. When Hawks hesitated, that worthy said softly, "Don't try it on, old man, unless you're ready for a one-way ride."

Hawks grinned. "Who the hell are you?"

"Name's Wyatt Earp," the tall man said and Hawks holstered his gun and nodded at the whiskey and asked, "Care to join me, Mr. Earp?"

Earp did not move. "You'll be Hitch Hawks," he said.

"That's my name," Hawks agreed.

Tapping his shirt front, Earp said, "Got some warrants here for some fellers. Name of Johnny Ringo, Pete Spencer, Bill Brocius and Phin Clanton."

Hawks shrugged. "I damn sure ain't got 'em hid in my chap pockets."

Earp did not smile. "These men are wanted for robbery and murder."

"Still ain't got no information for you, marshal . . . sorry."

Earp nodded, then said quietly, "Mr. Hawks, we got a name out here for a man who beats up a helpless drunk, and Charlie Summers is just that—a helpless drunk. Nobody in this part of the country takes him seriously, but if I was you, I'd get on my horse and ride to hell outa this town because the folks here happen to like him and they have a great deal of respect for his wife. They might just decide to hold a necktie party."

"To hell with them," Hawks said roughly, then Thorpe came in from the street and said, "Hitch, they's a bunch of folks gatherin' down by the church. Look kinda mad about something," and then he saw Earp and froze.

Earp smiled faintly and nodded at Thorpe, said, "Hello, T.J. How you?"

"Fine, marshal, fine," Thorpe said, glancing at Hawks.

Looking around at Thorpe, Hawks said, "Seems the marshal here is looking for some fellers. Wants 'em for murder."

"Anybody we know?" Thorpe asked, turning a chair around and sitting astraddle of it.

"Nope, just some local boys," and Hawks lifted his glass and drank it empty and then looked at Thorpe and asked, "You say they's some fellers down by the church?"

"Both men and women. They're looking up this way . . ."

At that moment, Ah Kee entered the saloon and nodding at Earp, said, "Marshal, I'm happy to see you in such excellent health," and went and stood in front of Hawks's table, smiled and bowed and said, "Mr. Hawks, I am sorry I'm late."

Looking at Earp, Hawks grunted, "That's all right. Let's you and me take a walk outside," and rising he led the Chinaman through the alcove and as he passed out onto the sidewalk, he glanced toward the church and smiled. About twenty men and women were standing around glaring toward the hotel as they talked among themselves.

Ah Kee looked that way and observed, "Those people seem upset."

"Probably because I laid out the feller who owns this hotel," Hawks said callously.

Ah Kee, his face expressionless, asked, "Why?"

"I don't like drunks wallering around over me . . ."

Nodding toward the crowd, Ah Kee, said, "They are coming this way."

"Let 'em. All they'll get from me is a belly full of hot lead," Hawks snapped as Earp stepped into the street, looked toward the church and grinned.

"See you in hell, Mr. Hawks," he said and went and mounted his horse and rode south.

Watching him go, Hawks observed, "I thought that

feller was finished in Arizona and here he is riding around free as a breeze with a pocket fulla warrants.''

"Mr. Earp's still a U.S. Marshal," Ah Kee pointed out.

Thorpe came around the hotel leading their horses and nodding at Ah Kee, said, "Maybe we best ride on outa here, fellers," and looked uneasily toward the rapidly approaching crowd.

Hesitating for a moment, Hawks shrugged, then said, "What the hell," and mounted and led Thorpe and Ah Kee south along the stage road toward Dragoon. Ahead they could just make out the tall shape of the marshal as he trotted his horse along the same road.

They were several hundred yards from the town when a shot was fired by someone in the crowd, which had now arrived in front of the hotel. Glancing back, Thorpe grunted, "Damn fool. Using a Winchester. Range too great."

Ah Kee turned to Hawks and said, "Another shipment of guns will be ready for you to pick up in four days. Same place, same time. But if I were you, Mr. Hawks, I'd take along enough men to assure you don't remain down there. Phillip Zermino has many relatives in that part of Mexico. They may resent your killing him and his men."

Staring at him, Hawks asked softly, "Now how the hell did you know that, Mister Chinaman?"

"Simple, Mr. Hawks. I have men working for you who also work for me."

Pulling in his horse, Hawks said, "Maybe I should just punch your ticket right here."

Ah Kee smiled softly. "Perhaps you'd best think that over. Where Phillip Zermino has many relatives in Mexico, my relatives here in Arizona are legend. You wouldn't live long after killing me."

Hawks grinned, pulled his gun and earing back the hammer, said, "Maybe we'll just find out how tough your relatives are."

Ah Kee, showing no fear, shrugged, "There's also the guns."

Hawks laughed. "Hell, I can get a contact for guns any time I want. I don't need you for that."

"You kill me, Mr. Hawks, and your so-called contacts will dry up and blow away like the tumbleweed, leaving you a handful of air and a thousand enemies among the Tong."

Even Hawks had heard of the Tongs, knew of the deadly vendettas they became embroiled in and how they never stopped until the intended victim was lying cold and dead with a hatchet sticking in his skull. In spite of himself, the thought of such men after him did not set well. Grinning, he holstered his pistol and said, "You've made your point, Chinaman," and nodding at the Dragoon cutoff, said, "Here's where we part."

Bowing from the saddle, Ah Kee smiled his inscrutable smile and said, softly, "There was another ace in this strange game, Mr. Hawks."

"Another ace?"

"Yes, another ace. I held it," and he pointed toward a low knob a hundred feet from where they sat their horses and six men stood up, rifles in hand. Motionless, they waited.

Staring up at them, Hawks scratched his head and said bemusedly, "Just goes to show you a feller can't trust heathens," and turning his horse, took the road to Mexico.

Just before he was out of earshot, Ah Kee called to him. "Mind the Apaches, Mr. Hawks. You are riding into Cochise's stronghold and he doesn't like intruders."

Hawks ignored him.

Wolf and Rebecca O'Brien had watched Bedlam ride from the fort in command of twenty-five men and wondered where he was going and what his mission was.

"You reckon he's going after our old friend, Samuels?" Wolf asked. They were lying in bed together in Rebecca's room and it was two hours after taps. It had been the first time they had managed to get together since they arrived at the fort and Rebecca missed having Wolf on instant beck and call. Being able to merely look at him and walk away and have him follow like a pet dog gave her a wonderful sense of power. Smiling as he pulled her over on top of him, she thought, And all I have to do to keep him my slave is to do with him what I'd have to do for a husband with a lot less compensation.

Grinning up at her, he said softly, "Lady, you done stole away my heart."

She smiled back, hiding her head against his shoulder so he couldn't read her eyes. "Maybe Bedlam's going after dear old dad," she said.

"What?"

"Bedlam. Maybe he's after father," she repeated.

"Possibly," Wolf said huskily and then she rolled away from him and when he would have pulled her back, said, "Not now, darling. We've got to make plans; find out what's going on . . ."

Resigned to doing without her attentions, Wolf grunted sourly and said, "I talked to the supply sergeant yesterday. He and I, we kinda split a bottle out behind the commissary. He told me the colonel outfitted for a month and that he carried three times the normal ration of ammo."

"Something very big," Rebecca mused.

"Could be a routine patrol, too, what with the 'Paches being shoved onto the San Carlos Reservation."

Sitting up in bed and ignoring the fact that the blanket had slipped down around her waist and that she was nude, she said excitedly, "Wolf, let's leave here and go to Phoenix. I know some of the men father has worked with over the years. I think I can find out exactly what's going on.''

Staring hungrily at her breasts, Wolf was at the point where he would have agreed to shoot it out with Doc Holliday for an hour of her favors. He just couldn't seem to get enough of her and he was beginning to worry. He knew she manipulated him outrageously, but he was helpless to do anything about it. I reckon I'm in love, he thought, and hated the idea.

''All right, we'll go to Phoenix,'' he agreed and only then did she come into his arms.

They left the fort with an escort to Benson, then boarded the stage there and made the long hard run into Phoenix, putting up at a hotel in separate rooms. Rebecca immediately went in search of her father, finally locating him at an exclusive men's club, where she had to send a doorman to fetch him.

After he had kissed her and shaken hands with Wolf, he said, ''What brings you to Phoenix? I thought you were at Bisbee with Aunt Maude.''

''I decided to come see you for a few days until the Army has the Apaches in charge again,'' she said.

''I was very sorry to hear about what happened at the Riverside Station,'' Burgess told her, silently wondering if the Magician had done his job as he had been paid to. He had not had a word from Leesville for several days and had begun to think something was wrong. He knew of Samuels's ambitions and had ordered his death because of them. Now here was his daughter with the gunman, Wolf, in tow. The senator was aware of his daughter's weakness for men and had deliberately hired Wolf as a bodyguard, knowing Rebecca would seduce him in short order. He did not like the thought of her loose morals, but had long ago given up trying to do anything about it. Like mother, like daughter, he had told himself, still bitter over his wife's betrayal with another man.

Rebecca smiled. "It all came out fine, thanks to that man they call Leatherhand. It seems he was responsible for getting us out of that mess."

Looking at Wolf, Burgess asked, "Mr. Wolf, what were you doing while all this was going on?"

"Trying to keep your daughter from being shot down while in the middle of a gunfight," he said. "If I had gone to the gun with that crowd, they would have punched my ticket and there's a good chance Rebecca . . . Miss Burgess would have been killed or injured."

Burgess did not miss Wolf's use of his daughter's first name. Now what do I do with these two, he wondered and decided to play it by ear. "Where are you staying?" he inquired.

"At the Maricopa Hotel," Rebecca said.

"I'll stop by this afternoon and we'll talk," Burgess promised, anxious to get rid of the couple and get back to the club, where he had been interrupted during a conference with several local politicians whose philosophies matched his.

Back at the hotel, Rebecca sat on the bed and stared out the window while Wolf, who had taken a room next door, paced back and forth, wondering what the hell he was doing in Phoenix.

Looking up at him, Rebecca asked curiously, "How much is my father paying you?"

Wolf stopped and stared at her. "Three hundred a month and expenses."

"My goodness, you are a very lucky young man," she said with a twinkle in her eye. "All that money and me in the bargain . . ."

Damn her, he thought, but had to agree she was right. It was a lot of money for one man to make and suddenly

Wolf wondered just why the hell Burgess was paying him so much. Watching his face, Rebecca smiled and said, ''So, it finally penetrated that handsome skull of yours, did it?''

Walking to the window he stared down into the street, then turned and asked, ''You got any idea why your paw's willing to shell out that kinda money just for a guard?''

Pretending to pout, she asked, ''Why dear me, don't you think I'm worth it?''

Shaking his head he said, ''Hell, I'd do it for nothing and you damn well know it. What I can't figure out is why he's doing it.''

Cocking her head to one side and opening her eyes as wide as she could, she said, ''You know what? Neither can I, but damnit, I'm going to find out.''

A faint knock at the door interrupted them and Rebecca walked over and opened it and found Mike Overly standing there.

''Hello, Miss O'Brien . . . or is it Burgess?'' he said.

Hand on his gun, Wolf suddenly metamorphosed into a cold-eyed killing machine in front of Rebecca's eyes and she marveled. It was the first time she had seen him in this role and it sent a thrill through her as she watched Overly's face suddenly turn grey under Wolf's cold appraisal.

''What can we do for you, Mr. Overly?'' Wolf asked.

''You could invite me in,'' he said.

Pulling the door wide, Rebecca said, ''Come in then, but I'd be very careful what you do with your hands, sir, as Mr. Wolf seems just a bit edgy. Perhaps it's because my father has tasked him with protecting me.''

''In that case, he has nothing to fear from me,'' Overly assured her. ''My interests probably lie with yours.''

Wolf looked at Rebecca then nodding at Overly's guns, said, ''Maybe you best toss those things over on the bed . . . just so Miss O'Brien feels more comfortable.''

Without hesitation, Overly complied, then went and took a chair near the wall as Rebecca closed and locked the door.

"Who are you, Mr. Overly?" she asked.

He smiled. "Me, I work for Wells Fargo."

Wolf stared at him. "An undercover agent," he said softly.

"That about sums it up," Overly said.

"What the hell could you want with us?"

Overly glanced at Rebecca and then cleared his throat. "It seems her father has some rather interesting plans which include robbing stagecoaches and a few banks . . . and the young lady is not included in those plans . . ."

Wolf started to protest, but Rebecca held up her hand and said, "Go on, Mr. Overly, you fascinate me."

Overly smiled. "I thought I might."

Chapter V

"You see, Miss Burgess, your father's aware of your anti-slavery philosophy and considering it's in direct opposition to his own beliefs, he made arrangements for Mr. Wolf to protect you and at the same time keep you from underfoot," Overly said.

Staring at him, her face a study in disbelief, Rebecca shook her head. "Oh no, not my father. He's a U.S. senator. Why, if the opposition party discovered he was in favor of slavery or even condoning it, they would run him out of office . . . they'd impeach him . . ."

"You are absolutely right, Miss Burgess," Overly agreed, "but he's been exceedingly careful. He keeps his distance from the actual rough stuff."

Wolf, who also seemed puzzled, asked, "What the hell does he figure to gain by getting involved with a bunch of pro-slavers. Hell, like Miss O'Brien says, all it can do is ruin him. They ain't no way the south's gonna rise again. It's whipped and tied to a post."

Overly nodded. "You're right. On the surface it looks like he hasn't a thing to gain and everything to lose. Look at it from another direction and you see the possibilities for considerable profit. Right now," and he looked at Rebecca, "your father has a small army of men up in the Pinaleno Mountains at a place called Leesville."

Holding up a cigar he asked, "May I smoke?" and when she nodded, tucked it between his full lips, fired it up and blew a cloud of smoke and said, "He needs money to pull off his grand plan, a plan that really doesn't exist. Samuels works for him. So does the Magician. Your father, the senator, has convinced these men they are involved because he plans to turn Arizona into a refuge for southern sympathizers wanted in other states for crimes such as murder and mayhem."

"The folks out here won't stand for it," Wolf declared.

Overly shook his head. "Have you noticed how many southerners there are in this state? Hell, almost three fourths of the population comes from southern states. They may be whipped but that doesn't mean they ain't still loyal to the south and southern philosophies."

"If there is no plan, what's my father involved for?" Rebecca asked reasonably.

"Money, plain old money," Overly said.

"But we've all the money we need," Rebecca protested. "Even if father ran out of his own money, there's always my inheritance, and I must say it's not small."

"It is now," Overly said. Reaching in a coat pocket he brought out a sheaf of legal-appearing documents, and handed them to her.

She read them carefully then looked at Wolf with a stricken expression and said, "These papers show father has gone through all of my inheritance—every dollar of it. I'm destitute."

Wolf took the documents and read them, then looked at Overly and asked, "What the hell did he use the money for?"

"He sank it in Arizona land," Overly said. "He's a speculator, a plunger. The only problem with the senator is

106

that when he runs out of money, he uses other folks' funds. Right now he owes a half million dollars, and his only assets are a dozen played-out mines, several thousand useless acres of cactus, and his home here in Phoenix. He even lost your home in Boston . . ."

Thinking about it Wolf came to a conclusion. "So, now he's going to use these pro-slavers to pull his chestnuts free of the fire. . . . They're gonna rob stages and banks and give him the money, figuring he's using it for the cause. He'll use it to clear his debts. . . . He's playing a damned dangerous game, the kind that'll get him killed," Wolf said grimly.

Overly nodded. "He's got Quade Garvey front-running for him and I figure if he gets between a rock and a hard place, he'll pin it on Garvey."

"So what's your roll in all this?" Wolf asked.

"If those pro-slavers start hitting stages and banks, Wells Fargo is in deep trouble," he replied. "The company's young out here and it can't stand a drain such as that would be. It could bankrupt us."

"I can understand that," Wolf said, but then asked, "How are you, one man, gonna head this thing off. Hell, man, they'll kill you so dead you'll think you was stillborn."

"That's why I came to you two," Overly said. "Miss Burgess, you know your father and I doubt that blood is thicker than water in this case, since he's left you a candidate for the poorhouse. Mr. Wolf, you have a certain expertise that could come in very handy in all this; you can use those guns you pack."

"Great," Rebecca said. "Three people against a couple of hundred. Wait until I go and order our tombstones . . . I'm going to have the inscription say, 'Here Lies Three Fools.' "

"We're not completely alone," Overly said. "My company has a number of top agents in the field. True, they're pretty busy, but we can call them out in an emergency such as this. . . . Then there's Marcus Bell . . .''

Wolf stared at him. ''What the hell has that butcher got to do with all this?''

''He's the anti-slaver faction's leader,'' Overly said.

Wolf rose and walked to the window and stared down into the street, then turned and asked, ''You mean there's two gangs involved here?''

Overly nodded.

Rebecca shook her head and muttered, ''My God, Marcus Bell. The man's a lunatic. They say he should have been hanged on the same scaffold with John Brown.''

Wolf said sharply, ''Me, I ain't about to get involved with a man like Bell, not for any amount of money.''

''What about allegiance to Miss Burgess?'' Overly asked.

''She knows where I stand with her,'' Wolf said defensively.

''You may find you have to defend her with your life,'' Overly warned.

''Who the hell's after her?'' Wolf asked, adding, ''They ain't nobody in Arizona knows she's Burgess's daughter.''

Overly smiled. ''I knew it.''

The man and the woman sat perfectly still and looked at each other, then Rebecca said softly, ''I think maybe it might be smart to join sides with Mr. Overly.''

Wolf nodded. ''I'm too far in now to quit, but it galls the hell outa my saddleback to allow Burgess to go on thinking he's foxed me.''

Overly looked at him and observed, ''Mr. Wolf, right now that's your best asset. As long as they figure you don't know what's going on, they'll not worry about you.''

''So what do we do now?'' Rebecca asked.

''Sit tight here at the hotel until I get back to you,'' Overly said.

"What you gonna do?" Wolf asked, not liking the idea of inaction.

Overly glanced out the window and then rose and walked to an ash tray and mashed out his cigar and said, "I'm gonna see if I can't find Leatherhand," and he smiled and let himself out.

Standing in the hall, Overly looked both ways and was satisfied he had not been eavesdropped on. When he left the building, he utilized a side door that let into an alley. Looking both directions here too, he saw no one and turned left and walked toward the rear of the hotel.

As he passed a doorway his eye caught the flicker of movement there and he turned just in time to take a hard-driven knife blade in his chest, grunted as it sliced upward, severing the nerves, muscles and finally penetrating the heart.

Staggering backward, he stared at his murderer, then in a last reflexive spasm, drew his right hand gun and fired directly into the body of the man in front of him, heard his dying scream as if from a great distance, then he was sliding down an endless black chute to nothingness.

When the shot hammered out from below, Wolf jumped to the window, raised it and leaned out. Below him a crowd was swiftly gathering around the bodies of two men. One of them was Overly.

Looking around at Rebecca, he said softly, "Scratch Mr. Overly. Somebody just punched his ticket."

"What?"

"He's laying down there in the alley as dead as a nit," Wolf said brutally.

"My God, what are we going to do?" she asked, her face white.

"We're going to get the hell outa this hotel trap and make a run for it," Wolf said and walking to the door, pulled it open and stared at the four men in the hall then drew with uncanny speed, leveled his gun on them and grated, "Move, bastards, and they'll be hammering dirt in your face."

Looking over his shoulder at the man behind him, the tall, grey-haired man in the lead said, "Now ain't this here feller being dramatic?"

The others chuckled, but their eyes remained cold and expressionless.

"Who the hell are you?" Wolf rapped out.

"Me, I'm Marcus Bell," the grey-haired man said, then jerking a thumb over his shoulder, added, "These fellers are workers in the vineyard of the north, as it were."

Wolf did not lower his gun. "What the hell you want here?"

"I have a proposition to offer Miss Burgess," Bell said smoothly.

"What's that? A knife in her guts like you did Overly?"

"Hardly, Mr. Wolf, besides, we didn't launch Mr. Overly on his maiden voyage to the nether depths," Bell declared. "He was done in by one of the Magician's people and not very efficiently either, I might add."

Wolf grinned. "I gotta agree with that. A man that gives his last breath for a cause ain't what I'd call smart."

"I take it you have no loyalties, Mr. Wolf?"

Nodding his head toward Rebecca, he said, "There stands my duty. Try to hurt her and you're dead."

"Understood, Mr. Wolf. Now may we come in? I'm not really all that comfortable standing out here in the hall."

Delta Kale didn't like the odds. It seemed that every time one of his men stuck his head out a door, he risked getting it blown off and now they needed water. Bedlam's forces had kept them bottled up in their cabins day and night. The first night the Magician had sent his people to the lake for water. Halfway there a huge ball of tumble-weeds rolled down the face of the cliff, flames pouring from them and lighting up the entire valley. Two men had died halfway between the town and its water supply. Now he couldn't get anybody else to try it for fear they would meet the same fate.

Sitting at the long dining room table in the headquarters building the Magician looked across at Garvey who sat drinking hot coffee, and observed, "Mr. Garvey, it appears we are caught in a trap of our own making."

Looking up, Garvey said disgustedly, "A fine bunch of fighters Samuels gathered. They got a Gatling gun out there and enough Spencers to fight the war all over again and we can't get one of them to leave his cabin."

Kale stood up and said, "I'm gonna make the rounds. See if I can pump some courage into these people," and he left by a rear door.

Walking quietly, for he knew sound carried a great distance in desert country, he made his way to the first cabin, pushed open the back door and found its occupant in bed with one of the camp girls.

Looking up, the man said, "Hey, what the hell . . ."

The girl, gazing wide-eyed past the man's shoulder, smiled and said nothing.

"How's your water supply?" Kale asked.

"Why, they ain't none," the outlaw answered.

"You figure on laying around here until you croak from thirst?"

Grinning, the man said, "Hell, you're the big he wampus here. It's up to you."

"Maybe you're right," Kale mused and left, closing the door quietly as the woman said something in a hushed voice.

He stopped at all the cabins on the west side of the valley and got much the same response. Knowing that he had better do something or he was going to lose the whole command, he picked up a bucket as he left the last cabin and walked quietly to the lake, filled it and carried it back. Stepping through the back door, he set it on a table and looking at the two men sharing the house, said, "All you gotta do to get water is walk down and get it," and left.

Before morning Kale had carried water to every cabin and daylight found him standing behind the Gatling, sighting along its tubular barrel. Garvey stood by as loader and when the first blue uniform showed itself on the cliff top, Kale began cranking the deadly machine gun, spraying lead along the lip of the overhang. His first pass was low but he angled it up as he moved the barrel from north to south and just as he reached the limits of his strafe, a trooper suddenly straightened up, took several rounds through the body and slowly tipped off the bluff to drop lifeless into the meadow.

Shouts and curses answered this action then half a dozen rifles opened up all along the cliff and Kale turned the deadly Gatling loose again, hammering slugs in a veritable stream along the lip of the bluff.

The rifles were suddenly silenced and turning to Garvey, Kale said, "Now!" and led the way at a hard run to the headquarters building. The first shots sounded as they bounded up the steps, then they were inside and flat on the floor as lead tore through the chinks in the wall, smashed already shattered windows, blowing glass shards across the room and sending bullet-punctured pots and pans clattering along the floor.

The barrage lasted a good minute, then suddenly stopped at someone's shouted command and crawling to a window, Kale carefully raised his head and looked out. His reward was a bullet that screamed through the opening so close to his head he heard it snap as it passed.

Ducking, he looked back at Garvey and observed, "They got a damn sharpshooter up there."

"Most armies have them," Garvey said dryly.

"Wish we did," the Magician countered.

Rolling on his back he dug out a cigar and calmly lit it, blew smoke at the ceiling and braced himself for a long day.

That afternoon the forces on the cliff fired the first cabin in Leesville. While the town lay quiet under the troopers' menacing guns, an arrow, its tip wrapped in rags, suddenly spiraled down from the cliff, trailing a plume of smoke. It buried itself in the roof of the southernmost cabin on the east side of the street and exploded, hurling flame all over the roof. In less than two minutes, the building was a raging inferno and its occupants ran from it toward a house on the west side of the street, only to fall beneath the deadly marksmanship of the troopers.

Peering through the front door of his headquarters, Kale watched the structure burn and witnessed the end of its occupants. His face a study in bitterness, he looked around at Garvey and said, "It appears we have inherited a very poor defensive position from Captain Samuels."

Garvey smiled and Kale suddenly liked him. At least he ain't afraid, he thought, then turned at the sound of another arrow striking wood and watched the shingles on yet another house burst into flame.

By full dark all the houses along the east side of the street were little more than gutted shells. From where he crouched against the wall peering through the door, the Magician counted eleven dead men. Two women had been allowed to cross the street to safety, but no man was spared.

"Kale!" a voice shouted from the bluff.

The Magician rose cautiously and standing against the wall near the door, shouted, "I'm here . . ."

"This is Colonel Bedlam," the voice called. "I'm going to allow the women to leave if they wish. If they decide to go, they can walk directly from the cabins and out through the pass, where they will be taken into custody by my men. They may take whatever belongings with them they can carry."

"What if they don't want to go?" Kale shouted.

"In that case, Mr. Kale, we will wait half an hour and from that time on, my men will recognize no gender," Bedlam shouted, the sound of his voice echoing from the canyon walls until it was almost distorted.

"All right, you women . . . You heard the colonel . . . You have my permission to leave and I'd advise it, unless you want to end up as a target in a shooting gallery."

Slowly the women came forth. There were fourteen of them and they carried their meager belongings wrapped in blankets or old clothes. Some of them had lost everything when their cabins on the east side of the street went up in flames. Watching them go, the Magician knew that tomorrow would be the end of Leesville. The colonel would sit up there and continue to fire his infernal fire bombs down into the buildings until all were torched and there was nowhere to hide. Leesville had indeed become a deadly trap. Once, when peering from a window, he had seen Vent Torrey near the edge of the cliff and cursed silently to himself.

Turning his head, he told Garvey, "As soon as it's full dark, I'm riding out of here."

"You're what?" Garvey asked.

"You heard me. I'm going out . . . right down the pass and right smack into that patrol guarding the entrance."

Garvey thought about it for a long moment then said, "Hell, I ain't got nothing to hold me here, I'll go along with you."

When full dark closed the valley off to prying eyes on

the cliff, the Magician led Garvey out the back door and along the rear of the houses on the west side of the street. The still-glowing coals of the burned out shells across the street highlighted their faces in demoniac caricatures of human countenances as they slipped from building to building and finally reached the horse corrals south of the last building. Quietly saddling their mounts, each man carried two canteens to the lake and filled them, then returned and led the horses to the entrance to the valley.

Handing his reins to Garvey, the Magician said, "Hold these," and entered the tunnel leading to the cliff dwellings, where he found the guard covering the lower canyon.

"Anything moving out there?" he asked.

The guard, a short, stocky Mexican wearing crossed shell bandoleers and toting a heavy Sharps buffalo gun, said, "They won't try getting through. They know better."

"You see any of them?"

"*Sí*, they have a squad down there. . . .Just enough to hold us into the bottle," the guard shrugged and the Magician could just see the movement in the pale light from a half moon.

"*Amigo*, me and Garvey are going to run that blockade," Kale said. "We are going out of here and get help and come back behind that cavalry troop and catch them flat up against the edge of the cliff. They won't have anywhere to go."

The Mexican slapped him on the back and whispered, "Good luck, *señor*," and the Magician returned to the valley, again told Garvey to wait, and followed the second tunnel to the cliff dwelling on the west side of the entrance and informed the guard he and Garvey would be riding out. He had no wish to be shot down by his own men.

Back at the entrance he told Garvey, "We won't mount until we're well past the guards then we climb aboard and hit it, and friend, I advise you to hit it hard because if you

don't, you'll have no more worries and Burgess will have
to find another aide.''

''I'm beginning to figure he's a madman anyway, trying
this,'' Garvey said sourly.

''Good luck, my friend,'' the Magician said and led
the way down the narrow cut.

They were almost free of the narrow rocky aperture,
when the Magician quietly mounted his horse and looking
back in the gloom, saw what Garvey was up too. Palming
his gun, he grinned to himself and slammed the hooks to
the big dun he was riding and, with a startled grunt, the
horse leaped forward and hit the ground running. There
was one bend and then they were into a stretch of sandy
trail and the fiery bloom of rifle shots came at them from
both sides of the cut. The Magician could hear the vicious
crack as lead struck rocks and moaned away on the night
wind to lose itself somewhere in the desert. Lifting his
gun, he fired at a flash and heard the shriek that denoted a
hit, then a body tumbled from the cliff side and rolled
limply into the trail behind him. Something tugged at his
coattail and his hat was whipped around on his head.
Screaming like a banshee gone berserk, Garvey roared up
beside him and, lifting his gun, triggered four shots toward
the east side of the cut and was answered by two blooms
of red-rose rifle explosions.

''I'm hit,'' Garvey cried and looking back, the Magician saw him sway wildly in the saddle, grab the horn and
right himself then they were free of the cut and breaking
across open desert. Half a dozen shots followed their
departure, but nothing came close.

The Magician did not let up until they were a good three
miles from the cut, knowing that as soon as men could be
detailed from the cliff top by Bedlam, they would be after
the two runners.

''How bad?'' Kale asked, riding in close beside Garvey.

"Gut shot," Garvey said bitterly.

"Damn, I'm sorry, my friend," and hooking his boot toe beneath Garvey's stirrup, suddenly heaved upward, hurling the wounded man to the dirt, where he hit with a grunt then lay still. Dismounting, Kale bent over the injured man and saw that his eyes were closed and said softly, "Can't leave you behind to talk and you're in too bad a shape to fetch along," and conjured up a long slim dagger. Placing the tip of the blade against Garvey's ribs, he moved it around until he found a gap and quickly thrust it deep. Garvey's eyes popped open, their whites showing luridly in the pale moonlight as he gasped, then a gout of blood poured from his wide-stretched mouth and the Magician jerked the knife free and stood away from his victim as the blood pumped his life away into the desert sand.

"Hell, you'd never have made it anyway, *compadre*," the Magician observed and stepping aboard his horse, picked up the reins of Garvey's mount and leading it, rode west.

Sergeant King awoke the colonel at three a.m. to inform him of the Magician's escape.

Staring at the young trooper who had brought the news from the valley trail, he asked, "How'd you know it was the Magician?"

"Saw him, sir. He bust right by me. Shot poor Henderson dead so close to me I felt the bullet hit him . . . It was the Magician all right . . ."

Dismissing the man and ordering him to eat and then get back to his post, Bedlam looked at King and asked, "Any idea where Nantaje is?"

"Carson there said the 'Pache was out scouting the west cliff when the Magician broke out. He went after him as soon as he got back."

"Damn! Go fetch Torrey and that Chinaman, sergeant,"

Bedlam ordered and, after the man had gone, rose from his cot and donned his pants and boots and pulled his blouse over his head. Strapping on his sidearm, he walked from the tent as Vent and Chan approached out of the darkness.

"Sergeant, get a fire going over here, will you?" Bedlam ordered, and heard the sergeant giving instructions, then two troopers appeared and while they waited, fetched wood and soon had a blaze going.

"Put some coffee on," the colonel ordered one of the men, then went and sat on a camp stool.

"What's happened?" Vent asked.

"The Magician and another man broke out of the valley; got clear away; killed one of my men," Bedlam said.

"The hell? Who was with him? Garvey?"

"Probably, but one of the boys told the sergeant he's sure he put lead in the second man," the colonel said.

"Nantaje?"

"Gone after the Magician," the colonel said and Vent knew the officer was worried. He had grown to like the Apache, just as Vent and Chan had.

Turning to Chan, Vent said, "Let's get the horses saddled. We're burning time," and nodding at the colonel, strode away.

Twenty minutes later he rode past the colonel's tent and nodding at the coffee pot, said, "Save some of that for me," and not waiting for an answer, turned south.

They found Garvey by following the circling buzzards. The sun had just tipped over the eastern crags of the Pinaleno Mountains and its fire struck ochre, red and yellow from the cliffs as they rode up a gentle slope and pulled in to stare down at Garvey's body. He lay sprawled on his back and the buzzards had already pecked out his eyes.

"Hell of a way for a man to go out," Chan observed.

Wordlessly, Vent dismounted and bent and examined

the body, then pulling the dead man's shirt back, stepped aside and allowed Chan a look.

"That Magician feller just don't like extra baggage," Chan said.

"This ties Leesville directly to Burgess," Vent said.

Chan nodded then examined the ground and noted the unshod hoof marks of Nantaje's horse and said, "The Apache's been here . . ."

They found Nantaje the next morning. He was lying behind a large boulder while his horse, its reins dragging, cropped grass nearby. Dismounting, Vent walked carefully around the boulder and looked down the barrel of the Indian's rifle and grinned. "Glad to see you're still with us, Nantaje," he said and meant it.

The Apache grinned and looked down at his leg and said, "Maybe Nantaje pretty soon croak. Pretty bad hole in leg. Damn magic feller smarter than Apache . . ."

Going to his horse, Vent dug first aid equipment from his saddlebags while Chan gave the Indian a drink of water. The wound was a nasty one, having torn through the lower leg just below the knee and breaking the bone as it passed on its way. Looking up at Chan, Vent said, "The Magician will have to wait. Our friend here needs a doctor," and he finished binding the wound after pouring a shot of whiskey into it. When the fiery liquid hit the raw hole, Nantaje merely looked up at Vent and said, "Damned white man wastes good whiskey."

Vent helped the Apache to his feet and half carrying, half walking him to his horse, helped him into the saddle while Chan retrieved the rifle and stuck it in the scabbard.

"You see which way the magic man went?" Vent asked, looking up at the inscrutable face of the Indian, who he knew had to be experiencing a considerable amount of pain.

"He go northwest toward Winchester Mountains," Nantaje said.

"Can he get water up there?" Chan asked.

"He probably go to Sierra Bonita Ranch. Him get water there . . ."

Nodding, Vent mounted and told Chan, "You take Nantaje here into Dragoon. Me, I think I'll just follow along and see where old Kale's heading."

Chan shook his head. Looking at the Apache, he said, "Feller's got him a death wish. Wants to die . . ."

Nantaje smiled. "My brother, he same way. Damned sum-bitch got married."

Vent laughed and Chan, grinning, led the Indian's horse away south. He did not look back, but merely waved a hand above his head. Vent watched the pair until the horses dropped into a swale, then turned the Appaloosa and headed north, commenting, "Old hoss, let's us get where we ain't."

Vent rode carefully, knowing the man he trailed was an old hand at this sort of game, even as he was. He would use every trick he had ever learned and Vent knew he had best come up with a few of his own. The advantage always lay with the man being pursued if the pursuer was a lone man. A posse could harass and push a man until he finally either gave out and turned and fought or tossed it in and let them take him. Vent had often wondered why a man who knew once he was captured he would stretch hemp surrendered. He had known them to do it and go quietly to their death, seemingly having accepted their fate even before giving up. He knew the Magician was no such man. Not only would he keep going, but even if Vent were accompanied by a posse, the man would be dangerous. He was the kind to turn back on you and start whittling down the odds, just as he, Vent, had done with Samuels.

Now he watched each rock, each cutbank and each cliff,

knowing his quarry could go to ground anywhere and shoot him from cover. This was an impossible country to trail a man through. Bare-limbed ironwood trees twisted their knarled limbs up from broken draws; huge boulders thrust spearlike sandstone from the desert floor. Huge saguaros, some of them thirty feet high, stood like green sentinels while their smaller versions all looked like human forms suddenly rising in front of Vent's horse. Twice he drew his gun only to discover he had mistaken one of these for the Magician.

At noon he rode into a wide, sweeping valley where organ pipe cactus grew in profusion. It made travel difficult and finally, not wanting to cut his horse up, Vent detoured around the valley, taking to a low ridge to the west even though he didn't like the idea of skylining himself. The move almost cost him his life.

He was half the length of the valley, his eyes shifting from one possible hiding place to another when the shot came. Vent was saved from instant death when his horse stepped into a low depression just as the shot was fired, pitching his body forward. He heard the vicious rip of the big slug as it parted the air inches from his left ear, then he jumped the horse off the side of the slope and, jerking free his rifle, landed running back up the hill. As he popped over the top, he caught a glimpse of a dun horse stretching full out across an open spot among the organ pipe, and lifting the rifle, sighted carefully and let drive at the dark-clad rider. As he fired the horse vanished behind a large cactus. Vent saw his slug rip a chunk out of one of its arms and cursed savagely.

Dropping flat, he snuggled the rifle to his shoulder and tracked it in the same direction the Magician had taken, hoping he would break into the clear again, giving Vent a clean shot. Instead, he seemed to have been swallowed up by the desert.

He waited half an hour, but nothing moved in the valley. Sliding back down the slope, he turned to stand up and found himself looking down the Magician's rifle barrel. Twisting violently to one side just as the gambler fired, Vent jerked up the rifle and got off his own shot, but Kale was gone, having dove behind a rock, leaving Vent in the open. Rolling sideways along the slope he cursed as thorns and sharp plants stabbed him in the back and hips, then he was behind his own rock and whirling toward where the Magician had disappeared.

Again he waited for a half an hour. When nothing moved near the rock, he carefully worked his way down-hill until he had a clear view of the backside of the boulder. The Magician was gone. As he rose and went to his horse, he heard the running thunder of a hard-driven horse and looking up, saw Kale galloping along the ridge, his rifle centering on Vent's chest. Diving behind a rock just as the Magician fired, Vent again missed death by scant inches. Whipping up his rifle, he fired at the running figure, knew he missed and fired again. Again he missed and then the Magician turned in the saddle and pounded off a shot, spun the rifle by its loading lever to seat another round and fired again. Both shots were uncomfortably close. Hunkering behind his rock, Vent glanced at the rifle and saw he had somehow bent the front sight out of alignment.

"No wonder I couldn't hit him," he said aloud and moved back down slope and found the Appy standing behind a palo verde tree, reins dragging, as he waited patiently for his master to get through with his loud games. Stepping into the saddle, Vent blessed the day Swift Wind, the Ute shaman, had presented him with the Appaloosa. He had saved the shaman's son from drowning and in turn Swift Wind gave him the horse. It was broke to stand and

Vent was sure that not even cannon fire would spook the big animal.

Looking up the slope, he gigged the horse and rode to the top, boldly skylining himself. He was certain the Magician, having failed to kill him this time, would ride on and wait for another opportunity.

Two days later, high in the Winchester Mountains, another factor entered the game. Following the Magician's trail along a narrow deer track, he suddenly pulled in and sat looking down at the unshod hoof marks of horses. They had angled down from higher up the slope and now they were following the deer trail.

Looking at the Appy's ears, Vent said, "Should let the 'Paches have him," then gigged the horse and rode on.

Marcus Bell's plan was a simple one. He had proposed that Rebecca go into hiding at a place Bell would provide and that he would then send a man to warn Burgess if he continued his efforts to create a secret army of southern sympathizers, his daughter would die.

Looking sour, Wolf observed, "The way I figure it, he'll probably tell them to go ahead and kill you."

Staring at him, Rebecca suddenly started to cry. Wolf went to her and putting his arm around her shoulders, said, "Aw hell, honey, I was only joshin'."

"No . . . you . . . weren't . . . ," she sobbed. Bell, who disliked crying women, walked to the window and staring down into the alley, remarked, "They've taken the bodies away."

Finally the girl stopped crying and Bell turned around and, evidencing more compassion than he really felt, said consolingly, "He won't let anything happen to you, Miss Burgess, don't worry."

"It's one way to head him off," Wolf declared.

"But then we'll all be broke," Rebecca said, appalled.

All her life she had had everything she wanted and when she grew into a bold, handsome young lady, men flocked around her, giving her a delightful choice of male companionship. And she loved men; all kinds of men. She knew she should get married, that sooner or later her indiscretions would become public knowledge and embarrass her father. Now, however, her dalliance with men seemed inconsequential compared to what her father was involved in.

"You may be broke, Miss Burgess, but at least the senator will still be among the living," Bell said ominously.

"What's that supposed to mean?" she asked.

"It simply means that if he continues to ride the same path, he'll be eliminated," Bell stated flatly. "We have no intention of seeing the rebellion continue here in Arizona. To make certain it doesn't, we'll cut off the head of the snake."

"You'd murder my father?" Rebecca asked, her eyes wide.

"As dead as last year's news," the white-haired antislaver said.

Looking at Wolf, Rebecca asked, "What should we do?"

Wolf strolled over to the opposite side of the room, then turned, and leaning casually against the wall, said, "We got us a couple of choices here; I can punch these old boys' tickets or we can go along with them or we can go our own way and play it by ear."

Bell glanced at his men, then looked at Wolf and asked curiously, "You really figure you could get us all?"

"Sure, Mr. Bell," Wolf assured him. "Me, I'm damned fast. You wanta find out how fast, why you just say the word and I'll start with you," and he dropped his hand to his gun and let it lay casually on the butt as he stared coldly into Bell's eyes.

"Damned if I don't believe you, Mr. Wolf," Bell said with a smile.

"You'd better believe me," Wolf said. He didn't relax.

One of Bell's men looked at Bell and said, "You want I should take this feller's belt up a notch?"

Wolf looked at him and grinned his lopsided grin and said softly, "They's eleven men laying under flowers who thought that. You wanta be the twelfth?"

Bell held up his hand and said, "Don't try him, Ev. He's as good as he says he is. I checked."

"Up to you," the man called Ev shrugged.

Half an hour later they quietly checked out of the hotel and entered a covered buggy and were whisked out of town on the road to Wickenburg. Five miles from Phoenix, Bell, who was driving the two-horse team while his men rode horses behind them, turned off the main stage road and into a narrow gulch leading east. The road here was little more than a trail, with sandy stretches denoting considerable water flow during flash floods brought about by sudden storms in the high country. They followed this road for two miles then entered a narrow canyon and eventually pulled up before a rough adobe house squatting against the face of a cliff. A corral just north of the house held five horses, the saddles for them draped over the corral fence. Several green trees and a swath of green grass indicated a spring near the corral.

Climbing down, Bell said, "They ain't nobody knows where this place is, Miss Burgess. Nobody comes here except our own people. Right now we use it as a way station when we need a change of horses."

A tall, lanky man wearing bib overalls, his cheek swollen with a huge chew of tobacco, came from the adobe and drawled, "Howdy, Mr. Bell. How you?"

Bell tossed the reins over the horses' heads and handed them to the man without answering him, then, while his men rode to the spring to drink and water their animals, motioned for Rebecca and Wolf to come inside. The adobe was surprisingly clean. There was a long main room which combined living quarters and a kitchen. A line of cupboards fastened to the wall were heavy with both canned and dried goods. The place had two bedrooms and Bell nodded toward one and said, "Miss Burgess, you can put your things in there and Mr. Wolf, you can use the other."

Wolf, who carried only a pair of saddlebags, went in and tossed them on the bunk and then came out and faced Bell. "What now?" he asked.

"We'll leave you folks here. Rufus will go back with us. I need him in town. I would ask only that you feed and water the stock each day for me. That was Rufus's job. With him gone, they'll need tending."

After Bell had left, Wolf went outside and looked around, noting they were as isolated as if they were in the middle of the Superstition Mountains.

"Nice place to get trapped by a bunch of Apaches," he told Rebecca when he went back inside.

She smiled at him, then taking his hand almost shyly, said in a low voice, "Let's go to my room. I need you very badly right now," and Wolf followed wordlessly after dropping the bar on the front door and pulling the rawhide latch string inside.

Chapter VI

Vent sat his horse and watched the line of Apaches moving along the valley floor, heading north. When the deer trail he had been following dropped down the side of the slope toward the valley, he stayed with the ridge instead and now had the advantage of height and a view that encompassed a radius of wild, jumbled country rough enough to give a mountain goat the queasies. The trail, even from this height, was easily discernable. It lay along the valley floor like a thin, brown snake, with no beginning and no end. Tracing the track with his eye, Vent saw that it followed the upward sweep of the north end of the valley, finally reaching a rifle sight pass and disappearing down the far side. As he watched, he saw a lone rider just topping out on the slope. He was leading one horse and riding a second and Vent knew he was watching the Magician. As near as he could estimate the gambler had about a three-mile lead on the Apaches.

Not enough, Vent thought, and gigged the Appaloosa into a trot. Following the top of the ridge by riding just below its skyline, he kept pace with the Indians, but was certain they hadn't spotted him. He could see that the ridge he followed eventually connected to a long line of peaks that made up the heights of the Winchesters and the gunsight pass the Magician had gone through was about four miles east of where his ridge met the peak line.

Vent figured he would gain a couple of miles on the Apaches when they started up the long grade to the pass because they would be forced to walk their horses on the slope whereas he could trot or even run the Appy along the almost flat-topped ridge.

He reached the peak line ahead of the Apaches and, instead of turning toward the pass, elected to ride along the shoulder of one of the craggy mountains and try to find a way down the other side. The slope was rocky, rough and dangerous and several times he was forced to dismount and lead the horse around some narrow point or between upthrust boulders. All around him the land appeared blasted and torn. Rocky outcroppings were jagged, torn and twisted by some upheaval of the distant past that had left the area tortured into weird shapes.

Looking around him, Vent had the eerie feeling he was on some other world. He had ridden in many strange lands during his wanderings, but this section of country was the strangest. Little wonder the Apaches had it all to themselves. It was a land that did not invite strangers to cross it. Only a man who had lived his life in this place, as had the Indians, would really feel at home here.

He finally made it around the shoulder of the mountain and found a continuation of the ridge he had approached this desolate land from and saw that it angled downward at a slight tilt, eventually flattening out on the distant desert floor. Down there it was a caldron of heat, cactus and more cactus. Looking at it from the advantage of height, Vent could see blind canyons that went nowhere; valleys rock-locked and inaccessible; spires of red rock reaching 300 feet in the air whose sheer walls reflected the afternoon sun in red shafts of light, and broad expanses of barren ground that would give a rattlesnake the shudders.

It was no place for a human being, yet far down the slope Vent made out the dark shape of the Magician riding one horse and leading the other.

Looking back along the north face of the peak line to where the gunsight pass cut its way through solid rock, he saw the first Apache come into view. While he sat there, one of them topped out on the trail and headed down the slope. It was plain they were not a hunting party, for even from this distance, Vent could see the streaks of warpaint. He estimated the distance between himself and the Apaches at about a mile as the crow flies, but in the clear mountain air of these ramparts, it was hard to estimate.

As he watched, the lead Indian, a tall brave wearing a red bandana, a buckskin shirt and dark pants, shoved his paint horse into a hard trot and the others strung out behind him. Deciding he needed more of a lead on them, Vent rode over the top of the ridge and found the ground on the west side fairly good going so he put the Appy to a gallop and, following the ridge just below the skyline, headed down toward the valley.

He beat the Indians to the flat and, as soon as he knew they couldn't see him, he angled the big horse northeast and kept him at a sharp gallop. Hidden by the rocks, he reached a low ridge he had spotted from the mountain and knew he was very close to the trail. Pulling his horse down to a careful walk, he allowed the Appaloosa to blow, then trotted him up the ridge side and reined in just below the skyline. Dismounting, he pulled his rifle free, dug spare shells from his saddlebags and crept to the ridge top and peered over.

Just below him the Magician squatted in a pile of boulders. He was staring along his back trail and from Vent's vantage point, the Missourian could see the Apaches were about a mile up the trail. Vent wondered if the Magician knew they were that close and doubted it. He had picketed his horses further along the slope, but within easy reach in case things went sour for him. Probably figures he can still run for it, Vent thought and settled down to wait.

Looking at the sun, he figured they had about three hours of daylight left and knew the Apaches, who entertained very few superstitions, however had one. They would not fight at night. If the Magician could hold out until dark, he could then leave and the Indians would wait until daylight to take up the chase.

Suddenly, they were there, riding into view around a huge rock. Watching, Vent saw the Magician raise his rifle, take careful aim and blow the leader off his horse. He fired five more times so rapidly, the shots almost blended into one. At the same instant Vent cut down three warriors, starting at the back of the column and working forward. When the smoke was blown away from that first encounter, he counted seven dead Apaches lying in the trail. The rest had vanished among the rocks like will-o'-the-wisps.

Vent was sure they were puzzled. He doubted they had spotted him, although he was certain they knew the Magician's approximate location. The Magician did not turn around and Vent wondered about that, then he saw one of the Apaches slipping up on the Magician's horses and taking careful aim, shot him through the chest. As the echo died against the distant peaks, four shots answered him from the rocks and instantly turned his hiding place into a den of flying slivers of rock. One of them grazed his forehead and left its bloody track and a second hit his left arm and turned it numb for a long moment.

Raising his head carefully, he was in time to see the Magician mounted and riding hard toward the north, having slipped away during the Apaches' barrage at Vent. Knowing there were only three of them left, Vent decided they posed no threat and ran for his horse. Swinging into the saddle, he raced him north, dropping down off the low ridge and onto the trail, which appeared closeup to have been well-traveled. He wondered if it was the track leading to the Sierra Bonita Ranch and the town of Bonita. If it was, there were three places the Magician could go for water and supplies; the towns of Bonita, Turkey Flat or the abandoned site of Fort Grant.

By studying his tracks, Vent could tell when the Magician slowed his horse to a trot. Vent too pulled in, wanting the Appy to be as fresh as possible if it came to a flat-out race. He was sure the big horse could outrun the Magician's horse, particularly if he continued to lead the second mount. Vent also knew that the man had been changing horses ever since he left Nantaje lying wounded behind the rock, and that might just give him the advantage he needed.

Thinking about it, Vent decided that even if the gambler outran him, he still had to go to ground somewhere for water and grub. When that happened, Vent promised himself, he would be there.

It was full dark when Vent pulled his horse off the trail and made a dry camp in a nest of rocks. He unsaddled the Appy but did not allow the big horse to run free, nor did he hobble him. Instead, he tied the animal to a stunted ironwood tree, rolled up in his blankets and was almost immediately asleep.

When he woke it was to the sound of voices and keeping his eyes closed, he lay perfectly still.

"Shore does look comfortable," somebody said and then Arkie Chan spoke: "Reckon he's cashed in his chips?"

The second man said, "Nope. He's breathing, but it's mighty weak."

Vent sat up and ignoring the two men, went and rustled up some wood, got the fire going, and poured water from one of his canteens into the coffeepot and shoved it on the coals. Glancing at Chan, he asked, "You got any coffee? I ran out."

The half-breed grinned and turned to Harp Denton and asked, "You got coffee, Harp?"

"Last time I saw you you were heading back for the home ranch," Vent said, looking at the cowboy.

Grinning, Denton jerked a thumb at Chan and replied, "This here feller came along and found me hunting strays east of the San Pedro. Said he didn't know the country. Wanted to hire me. When I found out he was your riding pard, I sorta volunteered to act as guide."

"Monger may be a little upset about that."

Denton shook his head. "I sent word back with another feller was with me. He didn't care to go hunt outlaws . . ."

Glancing at Chan as Denton dug out coffee and shook a handful into the now boiling water, Vent asked, "You make it to a doc with Nantaje all right?"

Chan nodded. "That damn 'Pache's got his share of hard bark. Never opened his mouth all the way to Dragoon. Only time he said anything was when we carried him into the doc's office then he wanted to know if the doc was going to give him some whiskey to ease the pain."

"You musta come a'hellin' after you left there," Vent said.

"I wanted to try and find your remains before the buzzards got to 'em . . . Give you a decent Christian burial and all . . ."

Vent grinned and told him, "You damn near had that chance. Old Kale, he's one foxy hombre. Almost put me under a couple of times."

"Looks like you caught a glancer?" Chan observed, staring at Vent's forehead.

"Rock splinters," Vent said. "Tangled with a bunch of Apaches back toward the mountains," and he told Chan and Denton how the Magician had run off and left him to face the Indians alone.

"Nice feller, that Magician," Denton observed.

"Now what?" Chan asked, as they drank coffee.

Turning to Denton, Vent asked, "How far to Bonita?"

Denton thought a moment then said, "Probably half a day's ride, give or take an hour or two."

Going to his bedroll, Vent put it together and tied it to the back of his saddle, then brought the Appaloosa up and quickly saddled him. Looking at Chan and Denton, he said, "Reckon we best roll. We're burning daylight," and watched Denton empty the coffee grounds on the fire then kick loose sand over it.

Handing Vent his coffeepot, he said, "Lead her off, Mr. Torrey. We'll stick to you like Siamese twins."

They rode into Bonita, which consisted of a store—saloon combination and an adjacent livery stable. A water trough near the corral was so full it had run over onto the ground and looking at it Vent thought, now that's a hell of a waste of water.

They let the horses drink then tied them to the corral and walked up the steps. As they were about to enter the store, Denton said, "Bill Bonney killed his first man here in '77."

"And he went down four years later," Chan volunteered.

"Always figured they put it on that boy," Vent remarked as they passed into the coolness of the store. He had once met the young outlaw near Lincoln, New Mexico, and had shared his camp coffee with him.

The store was empty except for the owner, a heavy set man sporting a walrus mustache and muttonchop whiskers. He had a single gunbelt strapped around his ample middle and carried two Lightning model Colts. They were the new self-cocking revolvers fast becoming popular among shopkeepers, bankers and gamblers because of their light weight and excellent stopping power at close range.

Planting both hands flat on the counter the store owner said, "Howdy, Harp. What brings you this side the mountain?"

Denton shook hands then nodded at his companions and said, "This tall feller is Vent Torrey and the other gent is Arkie Chan. Boys, meet Big Bill Randolph."

They shook hands and Randolph took his careful inventory of the two and looking at Denton, said, "You travel with some pretty hefty weight these days, Harp."

Denton grinned. "Nice quiet fellers, these boys . . . You got anything around here to drink besides that damned tarantula piss old Socks Canefield makes and tries to claim is whiskey?"

Randolph looked toward the door then said, "As a matter of fact there was another gent here not over two hours ago wanted good whiskey too. I wound up trading him a horse for one of his. Poor thing was done played out. Looked like it had covered some country. So did the man . . ."

Vent looked toward the front yard and observed, "This here country's sure hard on horses. You take that Appy of mine out there, why I've brought that horse over a hundred miles in the last coupla days. Poor critter's about done in."

Grinning, Randolph reached under the counter and came up with a dust-covered bottle and turning away, blew the dust from it and, filling three glasses, slid them in front of Vent and his friends and leaned back to await their reaction.

Denton raised his glass and said, "Here's to Lady Luck, Lady Mae and Lady Gay," and tossed it off, lowered the glass with considerable reverence and nodded. "Now that's damn good tonsil varnish."

Vent had to agree. It was good whiskey. Chan drank his

without comment, then asked Randolph, "They a back door in this place?"

Randolph stared at him, then said, "If you're looking for the toilet, they's a whole damn desert out there. Just walk aways out from the store, if you will."

Chan thanked him and found the back door. After he left, Denton said, "Damn whiskey goes right to a man's head. Reckon I'll drift out front and get some fresh air," and not waiting for Randolph to comment, walked out.

As the door swung shut, Randolph looked at Vent and asked, "Humor a feller, will you, Mr. Torrey? You boys trailing someone?"

Vent looked at the man for a moment then nodded. "The feller who traded horses with you? Was he dressed in black?"

Randolph nodded.

"Feller's an outlaw. Killed a feller over near the San Pedro. . . . Slit his guzzle . . ."

"I know him," Randolph interrupted. "They call him the Magician. A damn tough man and awful sudden with his guns."

"If you're worried about him maybe coming back after you, don't," Vent told him. "He's on his last ride."

"He'll leave some of you boys along the trail, Mr. Torrey, even as fast as you and your partner are," Randolph warned. "Denton, he's better than most with a gun, but he ain't no match for that feller."

"We'll keep him out of the line of fire," Vent promised.

"His lady will appreciate that. He's fixing to hitch up with Amy Jordan, over to Redington. Nice young gal. Reckon she'd rather attend a wedding than a funeral."

Vent grinned. "Thanks for the information. Didn't know he was about to get married," and he went and selected some canned goods, a side of bacon, two pounds of coffee

and a pound of flour and paid Randolph, then asked,
"You got ammunition?"

"What caliber?"

"Forty-four, thirty-eight forty and forty-five."

Randolph unlocked a cupboard near the end of the room
and came back and stacked half a dozen boxes of shells on
the bar and asked, "How many?"

Vent carried the grub and shells out and distributed them
evenly between his saddlebags and Chan's, then walked
quietly around the building and found Chan leaning against
the fence, looking at the horses.

When Vent moved up beside him, he said quietly, "I
got me a feeling. I think maybe our friend is watching us
right now . . ."

Vent had had the same feeling since riding into Bonita.
It wasn't the first time he had experienced such a warning.
Years of looking across his shoulder and down dark alleys
had instilled in him a sixth sense that screamed a warning
when something just wasn't as it should be. Looking
around now, he carefully checked the buildings, a water
tower behind the corral, a small shed north of the water
tower and an adobe that broiled in the sun three hundred
feet north of where they stood. Looking at it narrowly, he
said to Chan without looking at him, "Wonder what's in
that 'dobe?"

"Just what I was thinking," Chan said and then Denton
came around the building and looked at them and collapsed against the side of the store as his eyes rolled back
in his head. Sliding down the wall, he left a long smear of
blood to mark his fall and Vent and Chan, reacting instantly,
dove around the corner, guns in hand. Whirling, Vent
slammed five rapid shots into the open window of the
adobe and heard a shout then, as he punched out the
empties and reloaded, Chan fired at a swiftly running

figure that broke from the back door and disappeared almost instantly around a corner.

Vent ran out in front of the store, lifted his gun and caught a glimpse of the Magician driving headlong toward the north. As Vent fired, he disappeared in the brush almost directly in line with the adobe. Running for his horse, he suddenly remembered Denton and what Randolph had said about him getting married and swerved to the wall where Chan was bent over examining the cowboy.

Vent squatted and had his look and staring into Chan's eyes, asked, "How bad?"

"Knife. Got him high in the shoulder. He'll make her, but he's gonna need help," Chan answered then slowly stood up and punched the empties from his .45 and looking at Vent said, "I just wonder if Randolph knew our friend was waiting?"

Denton opened his eyes and said, "Bill's all right. He wouldn't throw down on a man. Knowed him for ten years. . . . How bad is it?"

"High shoulder cut," Vent assured him. "You'll live to marry that gal."

"Randolph musta told you about her," he said, and grinned.

"He did," and they helped the cowboy to his feet and half carried, half walked him inside the store and Randolph hurried around the counter and said, "Back here," and led the way to a bedroom where they eased the wounded man onto the bed.

"Bastard sneaked up on me," Denton said. "Slicker than any damn 'Pache I ever saw."

Looking at Randolph, Vent waited.

The store owner met his gaze unflinchingly and said, "I didn't know the feller was still here. Thought he pulled out, Mr. Torrey. That's God's fact . . ."

Vent nodded, then asked, "Who's in that 'dobe up the trail?"

"Nobody. It's been empty for quite awhile. I rent it out to a miner once in awhile, but nobody's been around for a coupla months."

"You here alone?" Chan asked.

"Not normally," Randolph replied. "Usually I got a couple of hired men here, but I sent them to Fort Grant for supplies."

Nodding at Denton, Vent asked, "You take care of this boy for us?"

"Hell yes. I knowed Harp for years. Me and him, we go way back. Know his boss and his lady and her family right well. Sure, I'll look after him."

They struck the Magician's trail three miles north of Bonita and found he had turned sharply west toward the Gila River.

Vent glanced back at Chan, who was studying the trail, and asked, "Any idea why our man would head for Florence?"

"Used to run a faro layout there in the Tunnel Saloon," Chan replied. "May have some friends there."

"Looks like one of his horses has come up lame," Vent noted and pulled up, stepped down and knelt to examine the tracks. Pointing to one hoof mark he said, "Notice how this one's lighter than the others? Reckon that old pony's favoring that off hind foot."

Chan had his look and nodded. "If he tries to hang on to that animal, it's going to slow him down considerable."

Remounted, Vent sat and contemplated the trail then mused, "You know, Arkie, I'm getting real tired of having that yahoo pick the ground. I figure it's about time you and I set up a little ambush for him."

"I'm listening," Chan said, watching Vent keenly.

"Let's take advantage of Mr. Kale's lame horse and see

if we can't cut around him; hit the San Pedro north of Redington and come into Florence from the south.''

Chan thought it over then observed, ''He'll probably follow the Aravaipa until he hits the Gila and then stay on the Gila to Florence. I figure that's about a two day ride. If we head south, cross the San Pedro at Redington then go north through Oracle we should be in Florence in a little over three days. He'll beat us.''

''Not if he keeps that lame horse, he won't,'' Vent said.

''He could just leave it,'' Chan suggested.

Vent shook his head. ''I don't think so. Right now he ain't got much in the way of assets. That old lame pony is an asset. He'll keep it because he's arrogant; he's a proud man. He doesn't figure us being a danger to him . . .''

''You may be right, but then he could drop that horse off at any one of a dozen ranches along the Gila,'' Chan pointed out.

''Then they's only one way to do this thing,'' Vent said. ''I'll break south for Redington and you stay on his trail . . . but Arkie, watch this gent. He's damned good. He almost nailed me, and I was lucky. So far he's taken Nantaje out and he's done for Harp. Both those fellers was good, specially the 'Pache.''

Chan nodded. ''I'll play it careful. I got me one or two more poker games to sit in,'' and he waved and rode on along the trail.

Pulling the Appy around, Vent pushed him to a hard trot and struck across country for Leach's Road and Redington.

Burgess sat across the table from Marcus Bell and tasted the bitter bile of defeat. Word had come that Leesville was no more and now Bell had just informed him that Rebecca was in the hands of the anti-slavers and being held somewhere. Bell was threatening to kill her and Wolf if he, Burgess, didn't resign from the Senate and leave

Arizona. Burgess had little doubt that Bell would carry out his threat; that he would kill Rebecca and merely consider it a part of the continuing war against slavery. Looking at him as the white-haired man sat there with his hands folded in front of him on the table, Burgess suddenly hated him more than anyone he had ever hated before and with that thought he calmly drew a .41 Derringer from his inside coat pocket and leveling it across the table, fired point-blank.

The heavy slug ripped into Bell's chest and knocked him over backwards onto the floor, the chair crashing away behind him.

"My God!" a man screamed, "he's murdered him," and as Burgess rose and fired the second barrel into Bell's body, half a dozen men rushed him and held his arms to his sides.

"Get the marshal," someone directed and a man rushed outside and returned within minutes with a lawman in tow. The marshal went straight to Bell, bent and examined him and then the wounded man opened his eyes and said in a whisper, "Made a mistake . . . didn't realize . . . man loved . . . his daughter . . . that . . . much," and then blood poured from his mouth and he seemed to sink into himself.

Rising to confront Burgess, the marshal said, "Sir, you've killed this man. He's dead. You'll have to come with me," and Burgess nodded numbly and when the man holding him released him, he straightened his clothes, handed the now empty Derringer to the marshal, and said, "I'm ready," and was led from the room.

As he passed out of the hotel, one of the men who had been with Bell at the hotel suddenly appeared and lifting a gun from beneath his coattails, shouted, "Damn you to hell, Burgess," and fired.

Burgess was turning toward the gunman when the first

slug hit him. As he fell back against the marshal, the lawman drew and tried to step clear for a clean shot, but the badly wounded senator had him blocked, then the Bell man fired three more times.

His bullets pounded into Burgess and the marshal, who screamed and collapsed, rolled over and cried out, "Ah God! I've been shot . . ."

Burgess, his upper body riddled, fell forward on his face, tried to rise, only to take yet another slug from the killer's gun, then he sank down and as his life's blood flowed along the sidewalk, died.

The gunman whirled and ran around the hotel as half a dozen men poured out of the lobby, guns in hand.

"There he goes," one of them shouted and lifting his gun, hammered off two shots. Both of them missed.

"Damnit, Ed, be careful," someone shouted. "They's women folks in that building next door . . ."

Lowering his gun the man ran around the corner, followed by two other armed men, only to catch a fleeting glimpse of a rider as he vanished down an alley.

When the chief marshal arrived he found three dead men, one of them a U.S. senator, one his deputy marshal and the third an infamous anti-slaver. Staring down at the two bodies in the street, he looked around and said tiredly, "Now this here's a damned mess if I ever saw one. Anybody calm enough to give me the whole story in fifty words or less?"

Half a dozen men tried to speak at once and the marshal held up his hand and said, "That's what I thought," and pointing at an elderly man standing near the back of the crowd, jerked his thumb toward the hotel lobby and ordered, "You come inside, Mr. Mosier, and tell me what happened. The rest of you wait out here."

The gunman, the man Bell had called Ev, struck the Wickenburg road and let his horse out to a hard run. He passed several rigs on the trail, but ignored their driver's cheery salutes and pushed on. When he reached the turnoff to the adobe where Rebecca and Wolf were holed up, he did not slacken his pace. Bursting into the yard at a gallop, he pulled the horse to a sliding stop and leaped down just as Rebecca opened the door.

"Where's your fancy gunman, Miss Burgess?" he called, watching the windows narrowly.

"Why?" she countered.

"Because I'm fixing to kill him, then I'm going to do the same for you," he said. His eyes were wild.

"Whatever for?" Rebecca asked, not understanding, but suddenly very frightened.

"I'll tell you why, lady . . . I just plugged your paw. He's as dead as he'll ever be. . . . Shot the double-dealing bastard right in front of the hotel," and the gunman suddenly began laughing, his face contorted horribly.

As Rebecca suddenly swayed, clutched the door jamb and then collapsed, a cold voice from behind the man said, "If that's true, you've killed your last man."

The gunman tried. He whirled and ripped out his .45 and was swinging it up when Wolf's first bullet took him in the chest. He never felt the second and third bullets as they tore into his stomach and throat.

"You tried, feller," Wolf said, but the gunman, face deep in the dust of the yard, never heard him.

When Rebecca awoke, she was lying on the bed and Wolf was bathing her face with a wet towel. Clutching his arm, she sat up and almost passed out again, then asked, "Did I dream that man?"

Wolf shook his head. "No, he was here . . ."

Looking around wildly, she asked, "Where did he go?"

"I reckon he's in some real hot spot right about now doing his best to duck the feller with the pitchfork," Wolf told her.

"You killed . . . killed him?"

"Deadern Adam's off ox," he replied.

"My God, my father . . ."

Helping her up, he said, "I reckon we better head for town and see what the hell's going on," and he walked into the front room, looked back at her, and asked, "You be all right while I saddle us some horses?"

"I'll be all right," she answered, but her eyes held a strange glitter and Wolf wondered as he went out.

They arrived at the hotel at the tag end of the marshal's investigation and seeing Rebecca entering the lobby, the lawman hurried over and removing his hat, said, "Miss, we've got us a shooting here and maybe you best find another hotel."

"I'm Rebecca Burgess," Rebecca told him. "I've been told my father has been murdered . . ."

"Hell, ma'am, begging your pardon, I reckon it's true. If you'll come sit down, I'll fill you in," and the lawman led the way across the room, glancing once at Wolf then ignoring him after that.

Settling on a couch Rebecca nodded at Wolf and said, "This is Mr. Wolf. He's my fiancé and protector," and Wolf stared at her then met the marshal's eyes as the lawman said, "I know Wolf, ma'am. . . . A lot of folks know Wolf. . . . Quite a few of them seem to develop a sudden case of death when he's around . . ."

Wolf smiled faintly and Rebecca looked at the marshal and said, "Please tell me what happened to my father."

When the marshal had filled them in, Rebecca stood up shakily and thanked the lawman, then looking at Wolf, said, "I think maybe we had best go from here."

Looking at her, the marshal asked, "Where will you go, Miss Burgess?"

Wolf answered for her. "The first place we're going is to the courthouse to get a marriage license, then we're going to hunt up the justice of the peace and get him to tie the knot.''

Rebecca stared into Wolf's eyes, then reached out and took his hand and he led her out.

Staring after them, the marshal replaced his hat and said, ''Now ain't that a whizzer for ya?''

They were married that afternoon and when they walked from the office of the justice of the peace, Rebecca gazed up at Wolf and asked, ''What now?''

Grinning, Wolf said, ''At least you know I didn't marry you for your money. . . . But then, I really don't need it. I got me a little spread down near Tucson; lays right spang up against the mountains there. Pretty good water supply, a few cows and some top grade hosses. Friend of mine works for me. Keeps things going while I'm away . . .''

Walking to where they left their borrowed horses, Wolf started to stop, then glanced at her and said out of the side of his mouth, ''Keep walking, honey. Somebody's watching these horses,'' and led her past, beginning a running description of the Tucson spread.

Once around the corner, he touched her arm and said, ''Go in that store and wait for me. I'm gonna see who's watching them ponies,'' and before she could protest, walked west then south, and returned along an alley. Halfway down it he saw a dark shape standing flush against the wall near the street and quietly walked up behind him. It was one of Bell's men.

Lifting his gun, Wolf placed the barrel against the back of the man's head and said softly, ''Move a heartbeat and you're history,'' and cocked the heavy pistol.

The man froze, then slowly raised his hands.

''Figuring on bushwacking us?'' Wolf asked conversationally.

''Hell no . . . just wanted to know who was riding our horses,'' the watcher choked out.

"We ain't interested in them worn-out nags," Wolf said, "but I'm gonna give you some advice that'll save your life, so you better listen up. Burgess, he's dead. So's your boss. I done for your pal, Ev. That don't leave much. Me and Miss Burgess just got hitched and we're riding out. If I see you or any of Bell's men following me, I'm going to arrange some sudden funerals. You *comprende*?"

"Hell yes. We don't want you folks anyway."

"I still think you're lying," Wolf said and pistol-whipped him and watched him collapse into the dirt of the alley floor with a soft groan.

Half an hour later, he and his new bride were riding the stage out of Phoenix, headed for Tucson.

Chapter VII

Florence wasn't much to look at. If it hadn't been for the Gila River, it probably wouldn't exist at all. The buildings were weatherbeaten and large sections of the plaster covering the adobe had fallen away, leaving the bare adobe bricks with their grass stuffing showing. Vent rode into the desert town with a great deal of caution. He had no idea whether he had outrun the Magician or not, or for that matter whether Chan had caught him before he reached town. Spotting a livery stable, he turned in and stepped down, dropping the reins and leaving the Appaloosa standing. Inside he found an elderly man with a long white beard and arms that had muscles like rope. Each time he lifted a hot shoe and drove at it with a heavy hammer, his arms bulged.

Looking up he laid the hammer on the anvil and wiping his hands on his apron, came out and nodded at Vent and asked, "Help you, friend?"

"Need this old pony watered, rubbed down and fed a bait of grain and some good hay," Vent replied.

"Want him stalled or turned out in the corral?"

"Stall him," Vent ordered.

"That'll cost you one dollar, mister . . ."

Vent dug out a silver cartwheel and handed it over then

asked, "Where can a man put on the feedbag in this town?"

Walking to the double doors the blacksmith lifted his hand and pointed toward a squat building down the street and said, "The Tunnel Saloon usually has a big pot of stew on and their whiskey's some better than most. They also got passable beer, although it sure ain't cool."

Vent thanked him and walked along the sidewalk, his hand never far from the .44, his eyes checking each doorway and alley. When he entered the saloon, he stepped to the right of the doorway, not wanting to remain with his body skylighted. Leaning against the wall, he waited until his eyes adjusted to the dim light, then moved down the room and stood against the far end of the bar.

A short, wide-shouldered man wearing a bowler hat and sporting a neatly trimmed beard and mustache, came along the plank and stopping in front of Vent, looked him over and saw a lean, brown-eyed man wearing chaps, a pair of worn Levis, a dark green shirt and a grey hat.

"What'll it be, mister?"

"Whiskey," Vent said and waited until the drink was delivered, then placed a dollar on the bar and watched the bowler-hatted bartender pick it up and place it between strong teeth and bite down on it. Satisfied it was real, he went and placed it in a box on the backbar and returned with Vent's change. Vent smiled and lifted the glass.

"Just stand right there, just like that," a voice ordered from behind him.

Looking into the bartender's eyes, Vent said softly, "You just bought a ticket to hell, friend," and then the man behind him snapped, "Up with the dewclaws. On top of your hat . . . Set the damn whiskey down first. No use wasting good whiskey."

Ignoring the order, Vent raised the glass and drank it off and observed, "I paid for it, I drink it."

"Well now, ain't he the feisty one?" the voice remarked.

Vent slowly turned around and at the same time raised his arms shoulder high and felt his gun being removed as the bartender leaned over and relieved him of it.

Standing six feet away was a runty cowboy wearing a torn and patched pair of chino chaps, a sagging brown coat that had seen better days and a roll-brimmed hat that had once been white. The man's face was lined and scarred, showing a lot of years of hard usage. The gun in his hand was a Russian .44 and he held it steady on Vent's stomach.

"Now, Mister Gunfighter, we see just how tough you are," he said, and Vent plucked the knife from its sheath and whirled it over his shoulder to bury it hilt-deep in the man's throat, moving with desperate speed to the right as the gunny fired his pistol in a spastic reaction to the slamming agony of a knife being driven into his jugular vein.

Whipping around, Vent saw the bartender's eyes suddenly bulge and realized the gunman's slug had ripped into the apron's chest and out the back, smashing a bottle on the backbar.

"Oh, my God," he said softly, and fell forward over the bar, his suddenly lax hand releasing Vent's .44. Stepping over, Vent caught the weapon as it dropped and turned in time to see the ragged gunman sink to his knees, his own gun forgotten as he raised a hand and pawed futilely at his throat.

"Not bad, not bad at all," a voice from the door said, and Vent swung his pistol and centered it on the speaker's stomach and saw the glitter of a star and waited.

"Easy there, Mr. Leatherhand," the lawman said. "I'm Marshal Philbin. Law in this here diggins."

"You buying a piece of this?" Vent asked.

"Hell no," the marshal said. "I ain't hankering to be buried with them two damn fools. I'm just an observer."

"How long you been there?"

"About two minutes," the lawman answered.

Long enough to have plugged me in the back, Vent though and holstered his gun.

"That piece of dog shit laying there on the floor with your blade in his guzzle was Dirty Sam McGinnis and the damn fool hanging over the plank was Poke Hazelton," the marshal said.

"How come?" Vent asked.

"The Magician rode in here three hours ago and hired these two addlepates to put you under. Said he'd do it himself but that he had some urgent business to tend to. . . . Now I know what that business was . . ."

Vent raised an inquiring eyebrow and waited.

"His business was to get as far away from you as he could and seeing what happened to these gents can't say as I blame him."

"Didn't happen to run onto a half-breed Chinaman around, did you?" Vent inquired.

"If you mean Arkie Chan, why he's down at my office waiting for you. Got him a little bullet nick, but appears to be able to ride . . ."

Walking to the dead man on the floor, Vent bent down and pulled the knife from his throat. It came away with a sucking sound and the marshal grimaced and observed, "Now that's a hell of a way for a man to cash in his hand."

Vent looked at him coldly. "Any way is a hell of a way to cash in," and nodded toward the door and said, "Lead off, marshal."

They found Chan sitting in the marshal's office with his feet up on a wood box sipping coffee liberally laced with whiskey. His left arm was in a sling and looking pointedly at it, Vent asked, "Caught ya napping, huh?"

Chan grinned sheepishly. "You were right. That feller's got more twists in him than a knot snake."

"He's also part cat. Got his share of lives," Vent observed.

"Heard shootin'?" Chan said, making it a question.

Vent went to the coffeepot and poured a cup and stood sipping it and looking over the rim. "Feller left two calling cards; the bartender and a snake by the name of McGinnis. I punched McGinnis's ticket and he up and shot the bartender . . ."

Chan stared at him. "Kinda careless of him, wasn't it?"

Philbin, sitting at his desk with his feet on top of it, grinned and said, "Old Poke, he just sorta turned out to be the innocent bystander," and he laughed and added, "I figured he was going to shove in his chips one of these days. Feller was always biting off more of a chaw than his mouth could hold."

"Any idea where the Magician lit out to?" Vent asked.

Philbin, digging around in his desk for his bottle, looked up and replied, "Headed south toward Tucson. Able Brown, he's a wood hauler, said he saw him riding hell for leather down the Tucson stage road."

Looking at Chan, Vent asked, "Arkie, can you ride all right?"

"I'm fine as frog's hair," Chan grinned. "He just pinked me. Took a little hide . . ."

"How'd he catch you?"

Chan stood up and walked to the window, then turned and said, "I spotted him about a mile ahead of me riding along the Gila. So, I sorta pushed my horse a little and then he turned and looked over his shoulder and lit out running. Me, I followed like a lamb to the slaughter. He went around a bend and simply doubled back and got behind me."

Vent shook his head. "You, my friend, are lucky you ain't learning to play a harp right about now."

"When he hit me with that rifle, it unloosened me from my saddle and the damned horse spooked and jumped out from under me just as he cut loose again."

"Well, Mr. Chan, I hope you gave your horse an extra bait of grain," Philbin grinned.

"I did," Chan replied.

Turning to the door, Vent said, "Let's get on the man's trail," then looked at Philbin and asked, "Marshal, if I had been just a little slow, or Hazelton hadn't caught McGinnis's slug, would you have taken a hand?"

"I reckon . . . but it wouldn't have been because I was helpin' you outa a jackpot. I just naturally didn't like Poke Hazelton," Philbin said, and grinned widely.

Looking at Chan, Vent observed, "You know, Arkie, I think this here hombre really means that . . ."

Chan smiled and replied, "So do I, Mr. Leatherhand, so do I," and followed Vent out onto the sidewalk and down to the stable.

Hitch Hawks was an unhappy man. He sat his horse among the rocks and jagged cliffs of the Sierrits Mountains and cursed in a low monotone. The rider who slouched tiredly in the saddle of the coyote dun looked away and wished he was back in Tombstone at the Oriental Palace watching the girls dance and sipping on a whiskey. This old man with his mangled hand scared the hell out of him. Hitch Hawks knew that.

Staring at him coldly, Hawks said again, "You mean to tell me the senator's dead, Garvey's dead and that gambler . . . what's his name . . . the Magician . . . is running for the hills? Is they anybody left alive who wants these damn guns?"

The messenger shook his head. "The whole thing is over. Hell, even Marcus Bell's dead, shot all to hell by the senator before one of Bell's boys did for him."

Looking back at the line of heavily laden mules, each with its twin wooden crates full of Spencer repeating rifles, he began to curse again, then looked around and watched T.J. Thorpe ride up the column. He stopped and talked briefly to a rider on the right flank and Hawks nodded in satisfaction as he watched the rider gig his horse into a run and sweep around a huge boulder on his way to mounting guard on the first high piece of ground he found.

When Thorpe rode up and pulled in his horse, Hawks nodded at the messenger and said sourly, "This gent says the army overran Leesville and Burgess and Garvey are both dead. Means we're stuck with $40,000 worth of damn rifles. Any ideas?"

Thorpe thought a minute then said, "Hell, I know an Injun, an Apache, who'd give us gold for the whole damn load."

The messenger, his eyes wide in horror, "My God, Mr. Hawks, you wouldn't do that? Give them heathens that many guns and they won't be a soul safe in this whole damn country."

Hawks shrugged. "Hell, me, I don't give a damn. This game's over. I'm riding out, but I ain't getting stuck with all these damn Spencers."

"The whole country will be looking for you, man. They'll surely catch and string you up. There won't be anyplace they won't look . . ."

Staring at him coldly, Hawks said, "One thing we don't need is a witness. You *vamos*, feller, and keep your mouth shut," and the messenger, his eyes filled with the knowledge that he had made a terrible error, one that he knew was going to cost him his life, nevertheless turned his horse about and said, "Your funeral, Mr. Hawks," and rode north.

Drawing his gun Hawks said, "Not my funeral, feller, yours," and lifting the .45, shot the man in the back and watched dispassionately as he was pitched forward over the shoulder of his horse to land in the dirt. The horse sidestepped when the rider fell, then walked on for twenty feet, stopped and looked back, its ears pushed forward in animal inquiry.

Riding up beside the fallen man, Hawks looked down into his pain-twisted face and said softly, "Last mistake, feller," and lifted the gun and shot again and watched the body jerk spastically as the heavy slug tore through the man's throat, blasting part of his backbone into the dust beneath his head.

Waving an arm he rode on and the mule train followed, each driver swinging his horse and the mules around the dead man. The last rider swung over and stepped down and removed the dead man's guns, checked his wallet and shook his head when all he turned up was a silver dollar, and mounted again and picked up the riderless horse and followed after the train.

Two days later, they camped at Verde Springs, a hideout for outlaws traveling from Arizona into Mexico. Horse and cow thieves moving stolen Mexican stock back into Arizona from south of the border also used it. There was a sizable lake in a shallow depression in the rocks fed by a sweetwater spring and backed against a cliff. An adobe cabin blended so well with the rock face, a man would miss it unless he rode right up to it.

Thorpe and two of his men checked it out with drawn guns while Hawks and a Papago Indian named Curly Chato rode around the campsite checking for recent tracks.

When Thorpe stepped from the cabin, he looked at Hawks, who was unsaddling his horse inside a rough pole corral habitually used by rustlers to alter brands, and shook his head.

Hawks dropped his saddle just outside the gate and while the rest of his crew pulled riggings from mounts, walked up the stone steps of the adobe and went inside. There was a crude Spanish-style fireplace built into one wall, a long wooden table made from split poles and covered with a flat piece of roofing tin, several chairs constructed from twisty pieces of ironwood and six crude bunks fastened to the walls along both sides of the room.

A fire was built in the fireplace, coffee added to a large pot of water and skillets full of deer steaks placed on top of an iron grill, where they sent off odors that filled the room, reminding the men they hadn't eaten since morning. One man mixed flour and water, added other ingredients and soon had a Dutch oven full of biscuits.

While the food cooked, Thorpe designated the men's guard mounts and warned them to stay awake.

"You go to sleep in this country and you just may never wake up again," he warned darkly.

When the food was ready the men ate, then four of them rose and went out and relieved the four then on guard duty, who came in and cleaned up the last of the meat, biscuits and gravy, then helped clear away the dishes and set them to one side for later washing. A deck of cards appeared and soon the men were playing poker, their faces lined with concentration as they studied their cards. Hawks, sitting on a bunk near the fire, watched them absentmindedly as he went over in his mind his next moves. He was well aware of what would happen if it was discovered that he sold repeating rifles to the Indians. He was also aware of what the Indians would do with them. He didn't give a damn. This was not his country and as soon as he sold the guns, he planned to take the money and leave. Never mind

154

that the original stake was put up by Burgess and Garvey. Hell, they were dead. This way, instead of receiving payment for delivering the guns, he would get paid for their value, a hell of a lot more money. Thinking about it and watching his men at their gambling he decided he would make a separate deal with the Apaches; once they had the guns part of the deal would be for them to kill off these border scum.

Thorpe came in then from checking the guard and the mules and leaning against the fireplace, said, "In the morning, I'll head out and see if I can make contact with the go-between. It shouldn't take me more than two to three days at the most, but just in case, allow me a week."

Hawks nodded. "I'll be working out a plan of exchange while you're gone."

Thorpe looked at Hawks and then turned his eyes to the fire, observing, "That ain't going to be the slickest part of this here deal by a long rifle shot. Me, I never saw a 'Pache yet I'd trust. Their middle name is cheat. Them bastards is slicker than a Mississippi River gambler."

"We'll just have to insist they come to a spot we pick and that they don't know about until they get there," Hawks said.

"How many should I bring along?"

Hawks thought a minute then said, "We've got us eight men 'sides you and me—that makes nine—so make sure they only bring eight men . . . and the gold."

The next morning Hawks rode out a mile with Thorpe then pulled in his horse and hooking a leg around the saddle horn, carefully rolled a cigarette left-handed. Watching him Thorpe said nothing, but Hawks knew the man was thinking of Vent Torrey and what he had done to Hawks's right hand on the platform of that lonely railroad station in the Colorado Rockies. Even now he could conjure up the image of that double-barreled shotgun with Torrey looking down those long tubes at him and his sons sprawled in death along the track, the victims of a Torrey's guns. I'm seventy-four years old, he thought, but I'll live to kill the last of the Torreys, then stuck the cigarette between his lips and accepted a light from Thorpe.

Looking up into his *segundo*'s eyes, he said quietly, "$40,000 split two ways is a hell of a lot more than split nine ways . . ."

As he let it hang there between them, he watched Thorpe narrowly, deciding that if the man showed the slightest indication that he was against the plan, he, Hawks, would kill him.

Thorpe grinned. "How we gonna do it?" was all he said.

"You're gonna arrange it as part of the deal," Hawks told him.

"You mean have the 'Paches kill 'em?"

Hawks grinned. His lined and brutal features resembled a death mask. "That's right. You tell your friend that as part of the deal he's to bring his men in to accept the guns then take care of the men he finds with them. In the meantime, you and I will have the gold and be on our way."

In the next three days Hawks stopped two fistfights and a near pistol duel between his men and, when he wasn't threatening them, he was sitting by the fire looking broodingly into the flames. While his men slept, snored and rose to man their guard posts, he remained seated by the fire. He had discovered that the older he got the less sleep he needed. He was beginning to notice another legacy borne with age: when the nights were cold, his joints ached and he knew that someday he was going to reach a point where he could no longer manipulate a .45 with his old swiftness and on that day, he would order his coffin, but he doubted he'd live that long. The fact that he had reached seventy-four, a ripe old age for a man living the kind of life he lived, never ceased to amaze him. Then he recalled the man called The Preacher who often traveled with Vent. Hell, he was over seventy and still going strong and they said he had been shot up no less than fourteen times. Well, he, Hawks, had a few scars to show as proof he had lived a damned reckless existence. Looking down ruefully at his right hand, with its remaining two fingers, he suddenly felt deep in his guts the bitter bile of what Torrey had done to him. The thought never entered his mind that he had contracted his own downfall. Hell, it hadn't been his doing that Torrey's gal friend got herself shot there in Crested Butte. Hadn't he paid a terrible price for that? His sons all dead and gone and now he the only Hawks left. Hell, at least Torrey had a sister. Thinking about her, he wondered why he had never tried to use her to get to Vent Torrey and then admitted it was all a matter of pride. If he couldn't take that damn pup by himself, he didn't deserve to win.

Looking at the mutilated hand again, he thought of all the hours he had put in practicing with his left hand. He had been lucky. Born almost ambidextrous, all it took was practice. From what he'd heard, Torrey still couldn't use his left hand; too slow. Vaguely he wondered why he really wore that leather contraption on his right hand. Hell, Hitch had heard the stories, but he didn't believe them. He figured the glove was sort of a good luck piece; that Torrey had used it until his hand got well and then because of the name, had just kept wearing it. That made more sense than the stories about the glove making Torrey one of the fastest men in the west with a gun.

I ain't about to try him face-on, Hawks thought. One thing he had learned in his long life; you didn't take on more tobacco than you could chaw at one time. Men who did that wound up choking to death. The fact that Torrey had allowed him to live after blowing away his hand galled Hawks worse than the killing of his sons. It was a damned insult. Why hadn't Torrey just finished the job?

The last guard mount before daylight went out and, half an hour later, as the sun tipped over the rim of the desert and sprayed its light across the cabin front, Thorpe rode in and slid tiredly from his horse, tramped inside and nodding to Hawks, helped himself to the coffee.

Hawks said nothing, merely looking at him and waiting.

Lifting the cup to his lips, Thorpe had his first sip then lowered it and said, "It's done. We meet with my man tomorrow at sunup in Five-Mile Canyon."

Hawks grinned his frosty grin and asked quietly, "And the other?"

"All taken care of," Thorpe replied and walked out and sat on the front steps.

Hawks followed along and stood leaning against the doorjamb, then thought, now I got to figure a way to kill you, my friend.

Thorpe, sipping his coffee and watching the sun rise, seemed oblivious to a double cross.

Vent and Chan rode into Tucson half an hour before full darkness claimed the desert night and, hunting up a livery stable, turned their mounts over to a Negro hostler and went in search of food, drink and a bed.

The food they found at a small restaurant near the town square. It was housed in a sprawling adobe that also contained a gunshop, saddlery, confectionary, notions shop and small hardware. Tramping to the back of the room, the two men took a table against the wall and each sat with his back away from the door.

Vent looked over the crowd and saw the usual group of

cowboys, miners, teamsters, gamblers and townsmen found in any frontier eating place. Absently he watched the waitress approach, noting her full body and tumbling red hair and felt a faint stirring and looked away. Stopping before them, she glanced at Chan curiously, then said in a deep, controlled voice, "Specialty tonight is beef stew and homemade apple pie."

Vent, looking into her green eyes, suddenly couldn't talk. As he watched, those eyes seemed to widen slowly and a flush crept up her neck and into her face and she said shakily, "We also . . . have steak . . ."

Chan smiled faintly. "We'll take the stew and two pieces of that pie," and nodding his head at Vent, said, "My addled friend here loves apple pie . . ."

She smiled then and Vent cursed under his breath and found his voice and staring directly at her, said, "Ma'am, I'll apologize now if I'm out of line, but you are the most beautiful woman I reckon I've ever seen," and his face was red and Chan was grinning even more broadly. Looking at him, Vent added, "If you, my oriental friend, make one single comment, I swear I'll shoot you right here in front of this lady."

The lady smiled and winked at Chan. "It appears your life is in danger, mister. Better not say a word . . . I'm Julia Ryan, gentlemen. Welcome to Tucson."

"Now how did you know we were strangers?" Vent asked.

"Why, that's easy," the woman replied. "You ordered the stew," and with a chuckle, walked away toward the kitchen, smiling at half a dozen men as they shouted greetings at her.

"Well, I'll be damned!" Vent exclaimed.

"I think she must have been kidding about the stew," Chan mused.

"It wasn't that," Vent shook his head. "That's the first

woman I've met since Lilly was killed that I've even noticed . . .''

Chan looked at him and observed, "It happens, Mr. Torrey, it really does happen."

When the Ryan woman brought the food, Vent looked at her boldly and asked, "Is it Miss or Mrs.?"

She smiled that devastating smile and said, "Why, it's Miss. It seems nobody wants me. Isn't that terrible?"

Chan grinned. "Now I wonder why? Could it be the stew?"

She tilted her head to one side and, fingertip at chin, looked at the ceiling and thought a moment and replied, "You may have hit on the cause, stranger . . ."

"Hey, Miss Julia," a man called from a table in the center of the room. "Need some more coffee over here."

Vent glanced at the man, meeting his eyes and the coffee drinker suddenly found something else to look at. Miss Ryan did not miss the byplay and wondering about it, took a closer look at her customer. She saw an average-appearing young man with regular features, maybe just a bit more handsome than most, and brown eyes and then she knew what it was; it was those eyes. Staring into them, she found only emptiness. They were as cold as the bottom of a hundred-foot well. Involuntarily she shivered and Vent read it all in her face and knew exactly what she was thinking.

Chan said, "My name is Arkie Chan and my friend here is Vent Torrey of Missouri," and both men watched her face and suddenly two men sitting at the table next to them jerked their heads around and stared at Vent and then looked at Arkie and abruptly got up and dropped a coin on the table and left. Watching them go, Miss Ryan looked puzzled.

"You fellers black plague carriers or something?" she asked.

Then she heard a ripple pass through the room and someone whispered in a too-loud voice the name "Leatherhand" and suddenly she knew and she stood quite still and then said softly, "Mr. Torrey, there's a play over at the opera house tonight. Have you ever been to a play?"

Vent smiled and nodded. "One or two; had trouble understanding what was going on, but I enjoyed them just the same."

"This one starts at eight and it seems I'm caught without an escort," she said, her eyes watching him.

"Why, that's downright awful, ma'am," Vent proclaimed. "We can't have that. This here's a right dangerous town, so I've been told. Wouldn't do for a young lady to have to walk the streets at night unescorted. I'd figure it a great favor if you'd allow me to escort you."

Smiling wider, she curtsied and said, "My goodness. I never would have guessed you would be interested. You may pick me up here at 7:30."

Before Vent could say a word, she was gone to wait on other customers and did not look around even when he and Chan finished their meal and dropped coins on the table and left with all eyes fastened on their backs. Outside on the street Vent said, "I need a drink," and led the way down the sidewalk and turned into the first saloon they came to.

It was well-lighted and bigger on the inside than it had looked to be from the sidewalk. A long bar took up one side of the room, which had to be at least fifty feet in length. There were five chandeliers hanging ten feet apart along the ceiling and behind the bar a full mirror reflected stacked bottles and glasses. Walking to a table near the wall, Vent took a chair that put his back to it and had his look at the place. There were three faro layouts, four poker tables going wide open and a keno setup. Chan, gazing around with delight, said, "I was wondering what I'd do while you were out courting a beautiful lady this evening. Now I know.''

''You might just check around and see if our man's been here,'' Vent suggested.

Chan nodded and then a waiter appeared and took their order and when the whiskey arrived, they sat with the glasses in front of them and watched the crowded room.

There were three men sitting at a table near the rear of the room who seemed to take more than a passing interest in the two gunfighters.

Vent looked at Chan and asked, ''You notice those three boys at the back of the room?''

''Yes, they seem to be kinda interested in us,'' Chan replied.

''Hard lookin' bunch . . . Seems I seen one of those jiggers somewhere,'' Vent mused.

''Which one?''

''The white-haired gent with all the hardware,'' Vent said.

Chan glanced casually around the room, then looking at Vent, nodded. ''That's Gene Buelah,'' and suddenly Vent remembered where he had seen him.

''He was at Leesville,'' he said, then wondered how the hell the man had managed to escape that bullet-riddled trap.

''Wonder if he left the same time the Magician made his jump?''

''No tracks,'' the half-breed pointed out.

''He could have slipped out quietly on foot in the excitement. A man with enough hard bark on him could make it to the San Pedro.''

''They's one thing for certain; he knows who we are,'' Chan said.

Then the men rose and quietly filed out without looking

162

at them and as soon as they cleared the door, Vent said, "Wait," and got up and followed them out and was in time to see them mount and ride north and thought, they're running. Afraid we'll turn them in to the Army, probably, and went back inside and sitting down, said, "They left. Rode north."

Nodding at one of the poker tables, Chan said, "Looks like a seat open. Reckon I'll give her a whirl."

Vent nodded. "When the play's over, and I deliver the lady to her lodgings, I'll come by here . . ."

"If I don't see you until morning, it'll be all right," Chan said with a tight grin.

Vent looked at him and said stiffly, "We Torreys was always gentlemen."

Chan stared at him, then observed, "Damn, you sure must lead a simple life," and got up and walked to a table and nodding at the dealer, asked, "Mind if I set in?"

The dealer, a white-haired veteran of the gambling fraternity, stared at Chan for a minute then said softly, "Arkie Chan," and the other players looked up and took the half-breed's inventory then looked away. Vent thought, at least that game will stay straight, and rose and left as Chan was dealt his first hand.

Out on the sidewalk, Vent walked south to where a sign proclaimed the building it hung from was a hotel and entered the lobby, signed the register and paid for two rooms.

The clerk accepted his money and handing over one of the keys, asked, "You want bathwater mister?" . . . and he spun the register and looked at the name scrawled there, and continued . . . "Torrey?"

Vent nodded. "Hot and plenty of it," and then he asked, "Is there a clothing store close by?"

The clerk pointed south and said, "Right down the

street,'' and Vent thanked him and turned and said over
his shoulder, ''You take the water up and I'll be right
back,'' and left.

When he returned he had several packages under his
arm and entering the room, he found a tub of very hot
water waiting. Locking the door and placing a chair under
the knob, he shucked out of his clothes and settled into the
big brass-bottomed tub and absorbed the heat of the water.
When he finally left the tub, he knew he had washed off
ten pounds of desert grime. Finished dressing, he actually
felt human again. He had purchased everything from the
skin out and had picked up his saddlebags while he was at
it and now he went to them and dug out his gun cleaning
equipment, sat at a small writing table and quickly stripped
and cleaned his .44. Using leather cleaner, he worked over
his holster and belt and then went to work on his boots.
Finally finished, he stood up and fully dressed, walked to
the mirror and examined himself and thought, now ain't
you some shuckins and for just a moment felt a twinge of
guilt as the proud face of the long-dead Lilly passed before
his mind's eye. Shrugging, he slipped on a short leather
jacket, looked at his chaps and spurs and finally decided
no man's wardrobe was complete without the gut hooks
and strapped them on.

On the sidewalk he dug out his money clip and checked
and grunted with satisfaction. The Army had paid him
expense money in advance and he had added it to his own
stake and if the lady cost him more than that, he reckoned
she might just be worth it.

He was half a block from the restaurant when the white-
haired man stepped from the sidewalk and moved to the
center of the street. One of the men who had been with
him in the saloon came from an alley directly ahead of
Vent and stood behind a porch support while the third man

stepped from a deep doorway on the east side of the street and stood behind a water trough.

Looking at them, Vent cursed under his breath and thought, well, there goes my evening to hell and moved out to the center of the street and stopped as Buelah raised a hand, palm outward.

"Far enough, Leatherhand," he called and at his words, the street suddenly emptied as men dodged into doorways or ducked into saloons.

The only sound along the street was the high tinkle of a rinky-dink piano playing 'My Darling Clementine' and Vent flipped the tiedown from his gun hammer and said softly, "Your play, Mr. Buelah," and waited.

"My play, you're dead," Buelah said and dove for his gun and Vent gave him no breaks, but conjured up the .44 and sent a bullet into the white-haired man's chest and spun and shot the second man loose from his porch support and swiveled again and downed the third man as he dove for cover behind the water trough.

Facing Buelah again, he heard the crash of the man's .45 at the same instant the bullet whipped past his face and he shot him again and watched the look of amazement wash across his face and then the man on the sidewalk, up on his knees, lifted his gun and Vent raised the .44, took careful aim and shot him between the eyes, blowing the top of his head off and pitching him into the dirt of the street.

Watching the water trough narrowly, he punched out his empties and quickly reloaded, then the man there rolled from cover and fired twice and Vent heard the smash of shattering glass behind him and shot the man in the face and suddenly something struck him in the back with terrible force and he was falling and even as he fell, he managed to turn and fire his gun empty as a dark shadow ducked down an alley and vanished just ahead of the vicious whipcrack of the tearing .44 slugs as they gouged pieces of adobe from the wall of the bank on the corner. Then the street came up and hit Vent in the face and vaguely he heard his name called and then his head was nestled in a soft lap and he was looking up at Miss Ryan and trying to tell her she was going to get blood all over her beautiful dress and Chan stopped, looked, whirled and grabbed a man by the arm and shouted, "Get a god-damned doctor, man," and ran for the alley, and as he passed, Vent saw the glint of the bared gun in his fist and wanted to shout at him to circle the building because he knew the Magician would be waiting at the end of the alley. But, Chan vanished and then Vent fell into a black pit, struggled futilely for a moment and finally, too tired to fight anymore, said distinctly, "Keep my gun for me," and watched her face swim away from him and turn to a vague patch of white and then disappear.

The Apache sat his horse near a palo verde tree and watched the white men approach. Behind him, eight braves sat or squatted on the ground and waited patiently. Hawks was sided by Thorpe and his Papago, Curly Chato. When they arrived at the palo verde, Hawks faced the mounted Indian and lifting a brand new Spencer from across his saddle, tossed it to him and watched quietly as the Apache examined it.

"You have seen the boxes of guns," Hawks made it a statement, not a question, for he had read the Indian's sign near the camp and knew they had been spying on the white men.

"I have seen them," he said.

"You have the gold?" Hawks asked, his voice almost bored. The Indian nodded toward a rock and Hawks looked that way and saw six buckskin bags sitting there and rode over and opened and hefted each one and then said, "The guns are at the cabin. All you have to do is go and get them.''

The Apache glanced at the Papago and the Indian interpreted Hawks's statement and the Apache nodded solemnly and then said something and Chato turned and looked at Hawks and said, ''He wants to know how he will stop the men at the cabin from killing him and his people.''

Hawks grinned frostily and said, ''Tell him all their ammunition has been taken away. Once they fire their pistols empty they will be helpless,'' and waited until the Papago spoke and then added, ''Tell him the ammunition for the Spencers is hidden in the rocks five hundred steps north of the spring.''

Once again Chato interpreted and Hawks waited. Then the Apache looked into Hawks's eyes and said in English, ''If you lie, old one, I and my people will follow you for a thousand suns and kill you.''

Hawks smiled. ''Speak English, huh?''

The Apache nodded and turned and rode away, leaving the gold on top of the rock. As soon as they were out of sight, Hawks rode over and picked up the bags and, unfastening his saddlebags, dropped them in and refastened them and then told Chato, ''You follow them. See what happens,'' and watched the Indian ride away and knew the Papago would be able to trail them when he had completed his observation. I'll kill him when he shows up, Hawks thought and turned and led Thorpe east. That night they camped at a small spring several miles from Tombstone.

It was full dark when Hawks said, ''Pee call,'' and rose and walked into the night. While he was gone Thorpe laid out his blankets and sat on them, his eyes probing the night.

When the shot came, he never heard it. The bullet entered his skull through his left eye and ripped a huge hole out the back and flattened itself against a rock. Thorpe's head snapped back and then sagged forward as his legs sprawled wide and chin on chest, he slowly relaxed. When Hawks walked into the firelight, Thorpe's right leg was twitching, then it stilled and the man was dead.

"Damn fool," Hawks observed and went and saddled his horse and mounted and rode toward Tombstone's lights, leaving the body where it lay. Hawks knew that this close to civilization someone would find the dead man within a couple of days.

He rode into Tombstone at ten o'clock and, tying his horse in front of the Oriental Palace, went in and took a chair near the back, paid for a bottle, and filling his glass, raised it and gazing through the amber fluid, decided if Chato caught up with him, he'd let the Papago live. Hell, the Indian knew this country. He might just come in handy and Hawks wasn't worried that Chato would demand a share of his new found wealth. Hawks had come to Tombstone purposely, for he had $15,000 on deposit here, money he had been paid for the last gun delivery. Together they made a sizable stake.

As he poured his second drink, he heard a man at a nearby table tell another man, "You should have been there, Pete. It was hell among the yearlin's. That feller Leatherhand, he punched them three gent's tickets so damn sudden they was dead afore they hit the ground."

"You say somebody plugged him from an alley?" the second man asked.

"Yep," the first man said. "Nailed him right after he put those three down. Reckon the back shooter was staked out there all the time."

"You figure Torrey will make it?"

Hawks held his breath as he waited for the answer, then the first man said, "He's got a better than average chance, the doc said."

Letting out his breath slowly, Hawks finished his drink and picking up the bottle, left the saloon.

Colonel Royce C. Bedlam was a satisfied man. He had shut down Leesville for all time, had either killed or captured most of the pro-slavers and when he returned to Fort Bowie, he had discovered the head of that snake was dead and so was the head of the anti-slavery faction. Their followers had scattered, those who weren't sitting in the Fort Bowie guardhouse.

Stepping up on the veranda of the officer's club, Bedlam started to open the door when his name was called and he turned and saw Speers coming across the parade ground. Waiting for him, he glanced toward the commandant's office and noted General Crook's black mule, the animal he called Apache, tied to the hitching post and surrounded by half a dozen Apache scouts. Nantaje was among them, but Bedlam knew he wouldn't be going out with the general, not with his wounded leg still unhealed.

Speers took him by the arm and walked him down to the end of the veranda and said quietly, "We just got word down from Tucson; Vent trailed that damned Magician all the way up to Florence then back down to Tucson and three of them slavers was waiting. Vent killed all three of them but somebody shot him from an alley . . . in the back . . ."

"Is he dead?"

Speers shook his head. "He was lucky. The slug missed his spine and instead broke a couple of ribs and deflected out his left side. It was a messy wound, but he'll make her."

"What about Arkie Chan?" Bedlam asked.

"He taken after the shooter, but lost him south of Tucson," Speers replied. "Arkie figures it was the Magician."

169

"Wonder if maybe we should bring Vent down here so the post surgeon can see to him," Bedlam said. "After all, he's working for us now."

Speers shook his head. "The doctor at Tucson knows his business. Vent's being looked after by the lady who runs the Yellow Rose restaurant there in town . . . Julia Ryan . . ."

Bedlam stared at the captain, then said, "I didn't know Vent knew her. Seems kind of odd, him and a woman. I always heard he refused to have anything to do with them since the death of the girl he planned to marry in Colorado."

Speers, whose reputation for chasing women was known from Fort Bowie to West Point, said, "Hell, the man's human, ain't he?"

"Sometimes I wonder," Bedlam reflected, and then looked up as the corporal of the guard, standing in the tower above the front gate, called, "Rider coming in," and the gate was thrown open and a young trooper, his right arm dangling bloodily, galloped through and pulled his horse to a stop in front of Crook's office just as the general stepped onto the porch pulling on his gauntlets.

"Sir," the trooper called, "A troop has been hit by Apaches near Five-Mile Canyon. They're pinned down there, sir. Injuns got repeating rifles," and he fell from the saddle just as Bedlam and Speers arrived in time to ease him to the ground.

Crook wheeled and shouted, "Bugler, sound assembly!" and the high, keening call of the bugle shattered the routine of the fort as men boiled from barracks, barns and work details and fell out on the parade ground to cries of, "Dress right; form up there; straighten up that line," and when Crook hurried onto the field and snapped, " 'Tench-hhhut!''

"Troops B and C, get mounted and prepared to ride,"

Crook shouted. "You'll need four days' rations and triple ammunition. Move it!"

When the men were assembled again and mounted, Crook, sitting his mule with his Apaches lined out behind him on wiry little desert horses, said, "We've just received word that Troop A is under siege by hostiles at Five-Mile Canyon. The Apaches are armed with Spencers. Let's go relieve them," and he whirled the mule and led the troops from the parade field at a stiff trot.

Chapter VIII

Vent swam upward from the dark well of his unconsciousness and opened his eyes to the harsh sunlight pouring through an open window. Slowly the events that put him here leaked back into his mind and then he shifted his position in the bed and a branding iron was suddenly applied to the small of his back and an arrow ripped through his chest. Gasping with sudden contractions of pain, he lay perfectly still and gritted his teeth against the subsiding waves of agony.

"You'll have to lay still if you expect to get well again," a soft voice admonished him and he slowly turned his head and found a pair of quiet green eyes filled with compassion fastened on his face.

Taking a very slow breath, Vent let it drain back out and said, "Where am I?" and then wondered why a man always asked that question when regaining consciousness.

"You are in my room, in my bed," Miss Ryan said.

Vent shook his head very carefully and observed, "Now that's a hell of a tough way to make it into a lady's bed," and went back to sleep.

When he awoke again it was dark outside and a small man wearing glasses on his nose was bending over examining his chest under the light of a lamp being held aloft by

Miss Ryan, who was wearing a green robe that set her eyes aglitter and made the highlights stand out in her mass of red hair.

"Am I going to live, Doc?" Vent asked, almost not caring.

"Ummm . . . probably," the little man said and straightening up nodded toward the bedstand and directed, "Put the light down over there, will you, Miss Ryan?"

She set the light down and came around the bed and lowering herself into a chair, watched him silently.

Removing his glasses the doctor dug out a large bandana and began methodically polishing them as he gazed at Vent. "Mr. Torrey, you have been very lucky, something I cannot say for the men who tried to kill you. They are all dead, but the slug that was meant to end your rather dubious career," and here he smiled frostily, "struck a couple of ribs and instead of blowing your heart into small pieces, exited out through your side on the same side of your body it entered. Left a nasty wound, but one you'll survive."

"May I have a drink?" Vent asked.

Miss Ryan rose and poured a glass full from a pitcher on the dresser and helped him hold up his head while he gulped it down.

"Dry," he said.

"You should be," the doctor told him. "You've been out for nine days."

Vent stared at him, then looking at Miss Ryan, shook his head as if refusing to accept the loss of that many days from his life and said, "I'm sorry, Miss Ryan, to have taken over your house and your bed. Couldn't you folks have moved me to a hotel or something?"

She shook her head. "That would have been impossible, besides, I'm a woman and women are natural nurses."

The doctor smiled his frosty smile and observed, "Miss

Ryan is my favorite nurse. I think sometimes she has more to do with getting a patient through than I do.''

''Probably decide to live when they get a good look at her,'' Vent noted, then knew his face must have been getting red and looked away as the doctor chuckled.

After the little medico left, Vent turned to Miss Ryan and asked, ''Arkie Chan . . . what happened to him?''

''Call me Julia, please,'' she ordered, then said, ''he returned three days ago. He's over to the saloon playing poker. Seems he's very good at playing poker. One of my customers at the restaurant told me he has won almost $10,000 since he's been back . . . He left word that as soon as you woke up I was to send for him.''

When Chan walked in, Vent was sitting up in bed eating a large bowl of Julia's soup, a pleased expression on his face. Looking up at the half-breed, he observed, ''Pretty soft living. Here I am, laying around at death's front door all shot to hell and my friend's sitting in a high-rolling poker game winning enough to buy a ranch.''

Chan pulled up a chair and straddled it, rested his arms on the back and laying his chin on his arms, gazed at Vent and said, ''Hell, I been trying to win enough to pay your doctor bill, and room and board.''

Vent grinned around the soup spoon and asked, ''That bad, huh?''

''Yep, doc comes high. Hell, he saved your butt.''

''He said if the slug hadn't hit a rib or two, I'd have been riding a cloud by now,'' Vent grunted, dripping soup down the front of his bandage-wrapped chest.

''Feller's sure sloppy,'' Chan observed.

''Only way to eat soup . . . What happened to the Magician?''

''Slipped south of the border,'' Chan said in disgust. ''Trailed the back-shooting bastard into Nogales and lost him when he crossed into Mexico. . . . Guess maybe I was being just a bit too careful. Me, I got a healthy respect for that gent.''

Vent nodded his understanding. "He's full of tricks, he is.''

"Something else . . . somebody's unloaded a whole passel of brand new Spencer repeaters to the Apaches. They been running wild. Burned out a rancher over in the Whetstones, killed a prospector down at Mescal Springs and hit the Chiricahua Cattle Company this side of Galeyville and killed a couple of riders and ran off a hundred head of prime beef."

Vent looked out the window and said thoughtfully, "New Spencers, huh? Wonder what Hawks did with that load of guns he was supposed to be bringing up from Mexico?''

"He wouldn't sell them things to the Apaches, would he? Hell, no white man'd do that.''

Vent looked at him and said coldly, "Hitch Hawks would. If ever a man don't give a damn for the rest of mankind, it's Hawks. Not only would he do it, but he'd think it was funny as hell.''

"If he did do it, I reckon we'll see if he thinks a hang rope is funny," Chan promised.

Then Julia came in and smiled at Chan and said, "Time's up, Mister Gambler. Mr. Torrey needs his rest,'' and she ushered the half-breed from the room, then came and sat beside Vent and taking his wrist, looked at her watch and began moving her lips silently as she counted his pulse.

"You'll never get a proper reading that way, Miss Ryan . . . Julia," Vent said.

Looking him directly in the eye, she smiled slowly and said, "It does seem a bit high. I think I'd best let the doctor do this. Wouldn't do for you to become over-excited . . .''

But she continued to take his pulse and when she finished, she went and wrote it down on a tablet lying on the dresser and then glanced over her shoulder at him and asked, "What will you do when you're well enough to travel again?"

Thinking about it, Vent suddenly realized the Magician just wasn't that damned important, but he also accepted the fact that he'd go after him simply because he could not leave such a job undone. To do so would be to leave one man out there who had back shot him and got away with it. Word would travel fast and Vent knew what that word would be. And because he knew, he also realized there could be no quitting when it came to the Magician, then wondered how he could explain all this to this lovely green-eyed woman with the soft lips and softer ways.

Before he could answer, she suddenly placed a finger on his mouth and said, "I think I understand. If you let this man escape, it would be an invitation to others. A man with your past cannot live long that way. Am I right?"

He took a deep breath and nodded. "You're right," and then he looked right at her and added, "Once there was a lady and I loved her and she loved me and we made plans and then she was dead because of a feud that I inherited from my family. She had no part of that feud, but she's dead just the same. I vowed then I'd never put another woman in that position. . . . It's going to be very hard to keep that promise now . . ."

She looked out the window for a long time then said very quietly, "I can understand that and accept it. At the risk of your thinking me shameless, I'm going to say something else. . . . I will always be available whenever you need me. . . . Do you understand what I'm saying?"

Turning his head he stared at her lovely profile and then replied just as quietly, "I've been lonely for a long time. It would be nice to have someone to come to when things weary me, but Julia, it's not a fair proposition for you."

Swinging her head then, she opened her green eyes

wide, and looking at him without a flicker of emotion on her face, said, "Let me be the judge of that. You're the only man I've met in years who I honestly wanted. I'm offering you a gift in return for what you can do for me. Don't turn me down . . ."

So they left it at that and spoke no more of it.

Bedlam led his hard-riding troopers south at a gallop and wondered how many miles the horses had in them at this pace. They would need them badly when they reached Five-Mile Canyon and he did not want exhausted animals under his men, but he also was driven by a great urgency to get there. The general had sent him on ahead with B Troop and his orders were explicit: Five-Mile Canyon by daylight tomorrow and no excuses.

Speers rode up beside him and said, "Colonel, some of the mounts are beginning to show the strain."

Turning in the saddle he looked along the line of blue-clad riders and decided Speers was right. "Order a trot, Captain Speers," Bedlam said and the order went back and Bedlam reined his mount down and held him at a sharp hand trot as one of the scouts came rounding in from the east and put his horse alongside Bedlam.

"Many horses cross trail three mile west . . . Injun pony," he said.

Nodding, Bedlam asked, "What you make of it, Pinto?"

" 'Paches heading for Five-Mile Canyon. Maybe so hear cavalry trapped. Want part of fight."

They crossed West Well at noon and rode over South Pass at four in the afternoon. At six o'clock, they galloped south along the Benson to Tombstone stage road, then curved off and crossed the road south of Mescal Springs. They camped on Babacomari River and were up at midnight and moving south again. As near as the colonel could estimate General Crook should be somewhere north of the Sulphur Springs Valley and just beginning the wide swing that would put him at the southern tip of Five-Mile Canyon, a wild, ragged crack in a long rocky ridge, the site of some ancient river that had long ago gone underground, leaving the canyon a blistered hell of rocks hot enough to fry eggs on, cactus, thornbrush and rattlesnake dens and no water.

The colonel led his troop through Camp Huachuca at early dawn and then pushed on to arrive just north of the canyon as the sun was tipping over the ridge to the east. As near as he could figure, they were about 10 miles south of the Clanton Ranch and twenty miles south of the milling town of Charleston.

Halting his troop, Bedlam sent out two of the scouts and gave permission for his men to dismount and rest their horses and kick the saddle kinks from their bodies. He wanted them fresh when he rode into that canyon.

When the scouts came galloping back to the troop, Bedlam waited patiently for them to dismount and squat in the dust then knelt in their circle and asked, "Well, Pinto?"

The chief scout, so named because his face was marred by a long slashing white birthmark that made him appear half-white, half-red, said, "They not fire now. Just wait. Troop in canyon. No water. Many horses dead. Men dead. Some Injuns dead . . ."

"Know who's leading them?"

Pinto nodded. "Bad feller name of Victorio. He plenty damn mean."

Bedlam stood up and looking at Speers, remarked, "We got our work cut out for us," and going to his saddlebags, dug out a map and motioning to Speers and Lieutenant Archibald Dinwiddie, a young West Pointer who had just been assigned to Crook's command, walked to a rock and sat down.

Looking at Speers, Bedlam said, "Duane, I want you

to take half the troop and ride around to where this side canyon heads up. According to this map, you should be able to take your men down it and slice into Victorio's flank, but use your scouts. Make sure they aren't guarding that pass.''

Bedlam allowed Speers half an hour to get positioned, then turned to his bugler and said quietly, ''Son, sound the charge,'' and the clear wild strains of the instrument carried across the desert and Bedlam drew in a huge breath, whipped out his saber, swung it high and put his horse to a dead run into the mouth of the canyon, his men hard behind him.

As they rushed headlong through the rocky slash, a sudden hail of fire poured down on them from the bluffs and now his men were answering with their handguns and the noise was fearsome. Men screamed and pitched from horses as Indians, shot through the body, came tumbling from their perches. Bedlam replaced his saber in its sheath and drawing his .45 Peacemaker, centered the sights on an Apache who was concentrating on firing at a running trooper who had been unhorsed, and shot him dead. Looking back, he saw Apaches boil from the rocks and begin dropping on his rear, pulling unsuspecting troopers from their mounts and dispatching them with vicious knife thrusts.

When there were at least twenty Apaches in the canyon to his rear, Bedlam suddenly shouted, ''Bugler, sound retreat,'' and wheeling his horse watched his men whirl and ride straight over the Indians, leaving all twenty dead on the canyon floor.

Turning, he shouted again, ''Bugler, sound the charge,'' and again the bugle called and the troopers whirled their mounts and galloped toward him.

Slamming the spurs to the big bay he rode, Bedlam led his troop around the bend and square into the middle of a vicious battle between Speers's troop and at least fifty

Apaches, all of them armed with repeating rifles. Bending low over the saddle, Bedlam roared in among them and shot an Apache in the face, saw him spin away and shot another through the back who was straddling a wounded trooper, knife raised.

Galloping on, he saw young Dinwiddie, his horse down and a ring of dead men around him, carefully aiming and firing as if he were on the range and thought, he's earned a citation, as he watched the troopers rally to the officer's position. Then the colonel's troop tore the Indian's position to hell and Bedlam, shouting orders, watched the Apaches swarm up the rocks and knew they were in the process of doing their vanishing act. He had seen it before. Unlike other tribes, the Apache fought to win and if he was losing, he would run away and live to fight tomorrow when the odds were better.

Wheeling his mount, he shot at a scrambling brave, saw blood blossom on the man's back and then Bedlam's horse grunted, staggered and began to fall and the colonel pulled his boots free of the stirrups and landed clear and ran to a rock and crouching there, continued to fire.

Suddenly, the distant sound of a bugler blowing charge came to him from down the canyon and he knew Crook had made it and marveled at the miles the general had had to travel, and the speed he must have traveled them, to reach this place now. Then Captain Speers wheeled in behind him leading another horse and shouted, "Colonel!" and Bedlam ran, shoved a foot into the stirrup and mounted and waving his arm, cried, "Dinwiddie, get mounted and bring your troop. Captain, clean up here," and as the lieutenant ran to a horse and swung up, led the troop south.

There was firing down there but it was sporadic and the colonel knew that the Apaches must have just about cleared out. He also knew they would split up and disappear like the dust in a windstorm and that no man could follow them, then he rounded a bend and pulled in his horse and walked him through the carnage of A Troop, or all that was left of it. There were dead men everywhere, but there were also dead Apaches, indicating Major Palmer Swain had sold his ground dearly.

He found the major lying against a rock, his left leg outstretched and bloody, a hole in the thigh covered by a crude bandage that was now soaked with red. Dismounting, Bedlam walked over and knelt beside Swain and looked at the leg and said, "Crook's coming in from the South. He'll have the surgeon with him."

Swain gritted his teeth and observed, "This was one helluva fight. The boys did all right . . . lost my exec and Sergeant Brandon . . ."

Bedlam nodded then rose and walked to his horse and stood by as Crook, sitting bolt upright in his McClellan saddle, rode into the ambush area and had his look and then directing a hard gaze on Bedlam, said, "Colonel, report."

"We haven't counted our dead and wounded yet, sir, nor have we counted the Apache dead. We just fought our way through to here, but the Indians have pulled off their usual disappearing act."

Crook nodded, then ordered, "Well, get your men about it. Let's clean up this mess and get our dead and wounded back to the fort."

Walking to where a young Apache lay, the colonel rolled him over, saw the hole in his bare chest and leaned down and retrieved the man's rifle and walked to the general and handed it up to him wordlessly.

"Brand new Spencer," Crook said. Bedlam knew if the general had been a cursing man, which he wasn't, he would now be turning the air blue. Instead he handed the rifle back and directed, "Gather every one of these up. I want them for evidence at a hanging trial."

Vent sat in a chair by the window and watched the street traffic then turned when Julia came in and said, "Hello, lady. How you?"

Smiling softly, she came to him and wordlessly bent and kissed him and Vent lifted a hand and placed it against her cheek and when she finally broke contact, said huskily, "You'd best be a little careful there, woman. I'm a man with a need . . ."

She laughed and as he watched the sparkle come to her eyes and the quick flush to her cheeks, he knew he would never forget this one, just as he could never forget Lilly.

"The doctor has informed me that you are not to indulge in strenuous activity," she said mischievously.

"I been playing possum on him," Vent said and reached and drew her into his lap and turning her head toward him, kissed her again as she slid her arms around his neck and returned the kiss with a great deal of fervor. When she broke, she moved back and looked into his eyes and said softly, "I'll come to you tonight," and rose and walked to the door, looked back with eyes wide and inquiring and was gone.

"Damn!" Vent said under his breath, then Chan came in and stared at him and said, "You look kinda feverish. Doc checked you today?"

"Go to hell," Vent said, and turned and gazed out the window again.

Chan grinned and sat on the bed. "Word just arrived from Tombstone; Crook's boys got caught in a snapper play down at Five-Mile Canyon. Apaches hit 'em with brand new repeaters . . . Killed twenty-two troopers and left thirty-four of their own behind . . . Hell of a fight . . ."

"Colonel Bedlam there?"

"Yep, led B Troop. Speers was with him too. Major Swain, he's the red-haired one, caught a slug in the leg. The major was in command of A Troop. They first got trapped down there and Crook led the others in to pull them out. Apaches faded away when the fight tilted against them."

Vent turned and looked at Chan and said, "I'm gonna have to take that old man out now. Should never have let him go in the first place."

"Hell, he killed your paw, didn't he?"

Vent nodded. "He did. He also killed both my brothers."

"Then I reckon it's time," Chan shrugged.

"You own the town yet?" Vent asked.

The half-breed grinned and shook his head. "So far I've whipped them for about $20,000 but hell, that may go tomorrow. Fact is, my luck's beginning to get tired. Been at it too long. Need to do something else for a while."

After Chan went out, Vent left the chair and standing at his full height, stretched his arms above his head, touched the ceiling and felt the slight pull of the muscles in his side and wondered what would have happened to his speed if the slug had hit him in the right side. Walking to the bed, he lifted his shell belt from a post and strapping it around his waist, noted he had dropped some weight and looked at himself in the mirror and saw a leaner face and a smaller waist, although his shoulders seemed to have stayed the same width.

Tying the holster to his leg, he stood up, suddenly dropped his leather-covered hand and the .44 seemed to leap into his fist of its own accord, hammer back and the bore steady on the center of his image in the mirror. Sometimes he was disconcerted by his own speed, wondering why he, of all the men he had met in his life, should have this uncanny gift.

Hell, he thought, sometimes I feel like the grim reaper

and reholstered the pistol, removed the belt, and hanging it over the bedpost, stretched out on top of the blankets and went to sleep.

When he awoke, it was to a presence in the darkened room, then he smelled the perfume and heard the soft rustle of clothing hitting the floor, followed by the soft sound of the door being locked. Sitting up he said nothing, merely removing his clothes quietly and sliding back onto the bed as she came into his arms with a soft sigh.

Curly Chato caught up with Hitch Hawks in the San Simon Valley. The old Missourian was camped in a dry wash when he heard the soft snick of unshod hooves coming from the south and slid into the brush and waited, his rifle trained on the camping area. Chato rode up, looked around, dismounted and squatting by the fire, helped himself to the coffee. Hawks came out then and nodding at the Papago, sat down against a boulder, laid his rifle to one side and retrieved his coffee cup.

"Many troopers die at Five-Mile Canyon," Chato said without preamble.

"Who killed them?" Hawks asked, but he really wasn't interested.

"Victorio's people. He is the one who got the guns."

"So he used them on the Army? Too bad . . ."

The Indian gulped half his coffee and observed, "Everybody goddamn mad now. Wanna hang feller who sell guns. Looky look everyplace."

Thinking about it, Hawks decided maybe it was time to move on. Go to Texas or back to Kansas. He still owned a place at Dodge City. Hell, with the money he had he could buy a string of really fine animals and go to trading again, just like he did when the boys were alive. Sooner or later Vent Torrey would come his way. The last of the Torrey

184

clan was a wanderer. A man in his profession had to be. He, Hawks, would get another chance at him.

"Army sending out patrols," Chato said suddenly. "Stop every man. Ask questions. Say they look for a feller named Hawks . . ."

The old man stared at the Indian and thought, damned heathen. Why didn't he say so in the first place and seriously thought about putting out his lights, but then decided it might not be healthy to fire a shot around here and risk bringing someone to check on it. Instead, he refilled his coffee cup and asked, "You know the route into Mexico, the one that crosses the desert where no man goes?"

"I know it, but it is great danger; no water . . ."

"That's where we go then, my friend," Hawks said and began breaking camp, planning to take advantage of the night.

Two days later, they were toiling up the ragged face of the western slopes of the Pelocillo Mountains, having dropped south to take advantage of an old trail Chato said was once used by rustlers to move stolen beef.

They were a mile from the pass when Hawks suddenly cursed and jerked his horse into a pile of boulders, followed closely by the Indian. Leaning over so he could see up the trail, he watched about twenty troopers drop from the ridge into the trail and knew they would find their tracks and be on them in a minute. Jerking his head down canyon, Hawks swung the horse and put him into a narrow defile that quickly hid them from the soldiers' eyes.

Two hours of hard riding and they were near the spot where Old Man Clanton and several of his men were cut down by Mexican ranchers, who it was said had caught them with stolen cattle. Hawks had heard the story and was more inclined to believe the job was done by Wyatt Earp and his friends.

Turning east again, he led the way into a deep canyon and was halfway through when he suddenly jerked his horse up as a slamming shot bounced its echoes off the canyon walls.

"What the hell?" he snarled and riding into a nearby cluster of boulders, said, "Chato, go see what the hell that was," and took the Indian's reins and watched him ghost away.

Half an hour crept by and then Chato materialized from a stand of ironwood trees and calmly walked to where Hawks waited. Nodding up the canyon he said, "Many sojers up there. Goddamn bluecoats wait in camp. Heard talk; say gonna catch feller who sell guns to Injuns . . ."

Thinking about it for a long time Hawks finally looked at Chato and asked, "You ever been to California?"

Chato shrugged. "One time. Go to steal horses."

Hawks grinned and then asked, "You know the trail outa Yuma?"

"I know him," Chato said. "Goddamn bad, that fellow. No water, just same here," and he swept his arm around in a semicircle.

Persisting, Hawks then asked, "You ever been to Tinajas Altas?"

Chato nodded. "Him pretty damn good spring, but many mans die there."

"Well, my friend, we're gonna drop into Mexico and then head for the El Camino del Diablo. Those bastards won't follow us there."

"I think maybe we die," Chato said and led the way out of the canyon.

Hawks grinned coldly.

They dodged patrols all the way into Mexico and once holed up for an hour while just over a nearby ridge the thunder of cavalry rifles came to them, indicating a sharp engagement was being fought. When the roar and rumble

186

of battle finally ended and they rode on south, they saw five Apaches traveling east. Two of them were obviously wounded. That night they crossed into Mexico and made for Fronteras, where Hawks planned to buy grub and a packhorse to carry it to Puerto Peñasco on the gulf. From there he and Chato would travel along the water to Golfo de Santa Clara, then angle north and cross the Colorado River just west of San Luis Rio Colorado.

They spent the night camped near a spring that Chato knew about, then rode into Fronteras the following morning. It was a mean scatter of adobe buildings, wide, dusty streets, stunted ironwood and palo verde trees, and everywhere they looked, dogs.

Riding carefully, eyes constantly sweeping the street and cataloguing every thing they saw, the two men reached a combination mercantile store and cantina and reined in and stepping down, tied the horses. Hawks turned to Chato and said, "Watch," and left him with the mounts and entered the building.

The proprietor, a fat Mexican sporting a walrus mustache, a wide grin and cold, calculating eyes looked up and said in English, "Welcome señor, to my humble store. What can I do for you?"

Hawks glanced at him then wordlessly went about gathering up a supply of grub while the fat one leaned on the counter and watched, a broom straw dangling from his lips.

Placing the items on the counter, Hawks asked, "Anybody got a packhorse for sale around here?"

The store owner cocked his head and smelling money, said, "A good pack animal, a tired pack animal or one that will die after twenty miles?"

Hawks stared at him then said softly, "A man ever sells me a packhorse that dies after twenty miles, he's going to wind up being buried in the same grave with the dead horse.''

''So, you want a good animal,'' the store owner agreed and now his grin was wider and his eyes even colder. ''I have the animal for you. He stands behind the store in a corral. You are welcome to go and look at him,'' and Hawks nodded and went through the building and walked to a rough pole corral and had his look, noted a brand that was well known in southern Arizona and grinning, re-entered the building to find a tall man wearing a star standing at the counter talking quietly to the owner.

When Hawks approached, he looked up and nodded, then said casually, ''Where do you come from, American?''

Hawks looked at him and then asked the store owner, ''How much for the packhorse and the grub?''

''I asked you a question, *gringo*,'' the Mexican said and dropped his hands to a pair of .45 Colts with fancy steer horn carving on the butt plates.

Hawks did not hesitate. He drew swiftly, rammed the barrel of his own gun into the policeman's stomach and pulled the trigger. As the man was slammed back against a stack of saddles, he turned and shot the store owner in the face as Chato burst through the door, his rifle up and ready.

''They's a packhorse out back,'' Hawks said calmly. ''Get him, throw one of these pack saddles on him and bring him around front,'' and not waiting to see if the Indian followed his orders, began carrying the food to the front veranda, where he stacked it in a neat pile.

Several villagers approached and standing twenty feet away, stared at him. One of them, apparently some kind of official or other, walked closer and asked, ''Señor, what has happened to the El Jefe and where is Pepe?''

Hawks ignored them. Leaning against a porch roof support, he calmly rolled a cigarette and when the Indian led the packhorse around the building and tied him to the hitchrack, began loading the food. When the load was neatly tucked into the pack bags and roped down, Hawks stepped aboard his horse and said, ''Bring him along,'' and rode west, leaving the villagers still standing in front of the store.

The Magician sat in a corner in the Coyote Cantina and sipped tequila. It was hot outside, but the breezes from the gulf cooled this small village fifty miles from the American border and all a man needed was money, an understanding of Spanish and the people who spoke it and life could be idyllic.

He had been in Puerto Peñasco for two weeks now and for some reason he couldn't define, had no inclination to move on. He had enough money, the owner of the Coyote Cantina was a good host, furnishing his gringo guest a small room in the back for a nominal fee and sent one of the village girls to him whenever he asked to be entertained. The fee for that service was also very reasonable. Although he found the food a bit too spicy for his taste, he was becoming used to it. Once, when Señor Hernandez asked him how long he would stay, he had looked at the Mexican lazily and said, ''Until the spirit moves me, my landlord friend.''

It hadn't moved him and even though he was occasionally visited by a small twinge of concern when he thought of the man called Leatherhand, whom he had been informed was still alive, he brushed it aside and played cards with Hernandez, Alfredo, the mayor and Gomez, the skipper of a large fishing boat that the Magician was sure was being used for other things than catching rock cod. Also sitting in the twice weekly game was an American named Bill Smith whose real name was anybody's guess.

189

Now Hernandez came to his table and inquired, "Cervesa, amigo?"

The Magician did not like the local beer. It was often flat, had almost no body and when you poured it, the foam took over the glass. Shaking his head he tilted the tequila bottle, filled his glass and tipping the neck toward Hernandez, raised an eyebrow. The Mexican probably weighed at least 260 pounds, and now he rose with great effort and waddled around the bar and returned with a glass. The Magician filled it and pushed the small bowl of lemon slices and the salt cellar over to him and watched him go through the ritual of sucking the lemon, licking salt from between his thumb and index finger and then tossing off the tequila.

Grinning, the Magician followed his example, then made the salt cellar vanish to the delight of Hernandez, whose interest in magic was almost childlike.

"Someday you will teach me that trick, señor?" Hernandez asked.

"Someday," the Magician promised.

As Hernandez watched, the Magician conjured up a silver dollar, deftly placed it on its edge on the table and then sat back and stared at it for a long moment. As he watched, the coin slowly began to rotate until it was spinning so fast it was a blur on the table. Raising a hand the Magician gestured and the coin stopped and seemed to hang there for a long moment, then began turning in the opposite direction. While it seemingly spun of its own accord, the Magician conjured up a second silver dollar and placed it flat side down on top of the spinning coin and it too began to revolve, but to Hernandez's astonishment, it twirled in the opposite direction. Watching it for awhile, the Magician grew bored with the trick and passing a hand over the two coins, made them vanish.

"May I ask you a question, señor?" Hernandez inquired hesitantly.

The Magician nodded.

"Do you use the . . . uhhh . . . tricks . . . when you play the cards?"

The Magician grinned and shook his head. "No, my friend, I trust to Lady Luck. She has always been with me. Let us hope she continues to sit behind my cantleboard."

"Has she ever abandoned you, señor?" the Mexican asked, helping himself to another shot of tequila.

The Magician shook his head. "No, but amigo, if she does, the Magician will be dead."

Chapter IX

Vent stepped from the saddle, and handing the reins to Chan, walked into the café. It was ten o'clock in the morning and the place was almost empty, but what customers were there looked around when Vent entered and continued to stare at him until his cold gaze met theirs then they turned away hastily and concentrated on the food before them, not wanting to irritate this quiet man who had killed three pistoleros in their town.

Walking around the counter, Vent went into the kitchen where he found Julia bent over the stove, her back to the door. Standing there for a long time, he watched her, then, apparently sensing his presence, she turned around and smiled at him, removed the heavy cotton gloves she wore to protect her hands from the heat of the stove, and came to him. Standing directly in front of him, she looked up and then gently placed her head on his shoulder, still not touching him with her body.

Vent put his arms around her and lifting her head with his left hand, kissed her gently, then more furiously, finally breaking away and moving back.

She still had her hands on his arms and looking at him with her wide green eyes, she asked, "You'll come again?"

"I'll return," he promised, then smiling, said, "Hell,

lady, I'd ride 500 miles for some of your apple pie . . .''

Still staring at him, she said, ''I'll always have some waiting for you,'' and her face got red and she walked to the window, pulled back the curtain and seeing Chan sitting on his horse, added, ''Tell Arkie good-bye and God-speed for me, will you?''

Vent walked to her and turned her and kissed her again and left and she continued to watch as he mounted his horse and rode downstreet, a tall man with cold brown eyes, broad shoulders and a right hand covered by a peculiar leather glove.

There goes my heart, she thought and only then did she allow herself to cry.

Vent said nothing as he rode south out of Tucson on the Benson stage road and Chan respected his silence.

They rode into Fort Bowie the next evening and Vent went immediately in search of Bedlam, while Chan took care of the horses. As the tall Missourian walked across the parade ground a voice called his name and he turned and saw a dark figure sitting on the veranda of the commander's office and turned that way, finding General Crook sitting there in an old rocking chair.

Stepping up on the porch Vent nodded, said, ''Sir, how are you?'' and waited.

''Sit down, Mr. Torrey, sit down,'' the general said and Vent eased down on a bench and the Fort Bowie commander, watching him, asked, ''Side still a bit tender?''

Vent grinned and his teeth flashed white in the pale light cast by a lantern hanging from the end of the veranda. ''Just a little, but we came a far piece since we left Tucson.''

''The Army owes you and Mr. Chan some money, you know?'' Crook said.

''I sure as hell didn't earn it when it came to the Magician,'' Vent replied ruefully.

"You did as much as any man could do . . . Almost got yourself killed trying to lay him by the heels . . ."

"I'm still going to bring him in or kill him," Vent promised.

"That's fine, but right now we're more interested in another fellow," Crook said.

"The gunrunner?" Vent guessed.

"The gunrunner," Crook agreed. "He's cost a lot of lives in this territory, no few of them from the ranks of my own command. I want him."

Vent looked across at the parade ground and noted Chan entering the sutler's store and asked, "You know who this man is?"

"We know and it appears he's an old antagonist of yours, Mr. Torrey. I'm told your family and his have been feuding for years . . ."

"Hitch Hawks," Vent said and then he looked at the general and asked, "You got a line on where he is?"

"He rode into Fronteras down in Mexico a week ago. Shot a town policeman and a store owner and made off with food and a packhorse. Had a Papago with him name of Curly Chato. Nantaje says he's bad medicine."

"So he could be anywhere?" Vent said.

"He was heading toward Puerto Peñasco on the gulf. The Rurales chased him into the mountains, but he slipped them. I figure he'll turn up at Puerto Peñasco, reoutfit and head for California since we've effectively cut off all other escape routes."

Vent thought about it then said, "They's a good trail from the gulf around the upper end of it and into San Luis on the Colorado. You got anybody out there, General?"

Vent could see the commander shake his head in the dark then he said, "I've deliberately left that route unguarded. He's yours if you want him . . ."

Vent turned and watched Chan approach, the glow of a

194

freshly purchased cigar throwing back its pale light to set off his strange oriental eyes and said, "Any word on the Magician?"

Crook chuckled. "He's hiding at Puerto Peñasco. Been there two weeks . . ."

"So, two fish in the same barrel," Vent observed as Chan stepped up on the veranda, said, "Evenin', General," and leaning against the porch rail, drew comfortably on his cigar.

Vent looked at him and said, "General says the Magician and Hawks are both at Puerto Peñasco. Feel like a visit to old Mexico?"

"They together?" Chan asked.

Vent shook his head. "Not yet . . ."

"Now that would be a tough nut to crack," the half-breed observed.

"Hawks is an easy kill if he'll face a man, but that ain't his way," Vent said. "He likes to shoot from ambush . . ."

Chan nodded, then said drily, "Seems to me he and the Magician have something in common."

Turning to the general, Vent asked, "Can we get quarters here tonight," and was told to check with the duty officer.

"Tell the captain I said to furnish you a private room," Crook said, then asked, "When will you leave?"

"Tomorrow morning," Vent replied and stood up.

"I'll see that the sutler has orders to outfit you," Crook promised. "You'll need a packhorse and several days rations."

As they went in search of the duty officer, Vent looked back and Crook was sitting there, his body still unmoving. I wonder what it'd be like to have all the lives in this territory in the palm of my hand, he asked himself, then decided he wouldn't like it.

That night he dreamed he was tied to a chair and the

Magician and Hawks were taking turns torturing Julia and he awoke with a cry, cold sweat bathing his face and chest and sat up as Chan, roused by the noise, crawled from his blankets and lit the lamp. Looking at Vent, who was now sitting up, he asked, "Ghosts come to call?"

"Something like that," Vent said, and Chan dug a bottle from his saddlebags and poured a generous shot into a glass and handed it to Vent. "Sleeping draught," he said with a grin.

The next morning they outfitted at the sutlers and drew a packhorse from the army remounts. When the sergeant in charge asked them if they wanted a mule, Vent shook his head. "No thanks, sergeant. We're going to be moving fast and if we happened to run outa grub, I much prefer horse meat to mule meat."

His face expressionless, the sergeant said, "I was with the General in '76 up in Dakota Territory," and went to cut out a packhorse.

Vent had heard of Crook's now infamous Starvation March in which he tracked a large band of Sioux from the scene of an engagement at Rosebud Creek through Wyoming into Montana and finally to Dakota Territory and the Dakota Badlands. Over 500 horses and mules were shot and eaten and for weeks the only food the men had were wild onions, berries, and their own pack mules and mounts and even they were so emaciated as to provide little in sustenance. It required over a month for the troopers to get back in shape again.

Vent and Chan left the fort an hour after sunrise and rode south, planning on turning west at the town of Cochise, then through Dragoon and finally Charleston, where they would replenish their water supply on the San Pedro River. The next leg of the journey would see them around the north end of the Huachuca Mountains and across the Nogales-Tucson stage road.

Their next stop would be Covered Wells, then Vent planned to turn southwest and make for Lukeville on the Mexican border. From there a trail led south to Puerto Peñasco and the gulf.

Vent recognized the fact that the trip was a long and dangerous one, made more perilous by the roaming bands of Apaches that were plaguing the countryside.

It was a country where the temperatures hit 110 degrees during the day and forty degrees at night. Any man traveling that land faced the unpleasant prospect of alternately broiling in the sun and freezing at night. This time of year, Vent knew, there was very little water, particularly on the final leg of their journey. Between Cochise and the Huachucas, water could be found at any ranch and there were many of them. There were also several small towns scattered along the route, each with its well in the town square and each with mercantiles where food supplies could be replenished. Beyond the Huachucas was no-man's-land for not even the Apaches could lay claim to it. It belonged to the snakes, the lizards, the horned toads and the roadrunners.

Crook had offered to furnish Vent and Chan a cavalry escort as far as Lukeville, but Vent decided against it, explaining that to do so would be to warn Hawks and the Magician ahead of time, for the desert telegraph was wonderfully efficient and news would proceed them, particularly if they were accompanied by a troop of cavalry.

"Cavalry might also provoke a fight with the Apaches," Vent said, adding, "The two of us will have a better chance of making it . . . besides, I happen to know Victorio. We are friends . . ."

Crook, a man with his share of Indian friends, stared at Vent, then observed, "I didn't think that fellow had any friends among the whites."

Vent had met the Indian chief while recuperating in a

cave near Dragoon. Victorio's sister, a prostitute who worked her profession from a small cabin in the hills, had found Vent after a savage running gunfight he had had near Tombstone the year before and had taken him in. It was while recuperating from his wounds that he met Victorio and later the Indian helped him clean out a bandits' nest at Charleston. Now, the chief was on the warpath and armed with brand new Spencers sold him by Hitch Hawks. Still, Vent knew enough about Indians to know that if they called you friend and you did nothing to betray them, they stayed your friend. He was banking on this if he came up against any of Victorio's people.

They rode through a silent and serene Cochise at nine o'clock that evening and turned west to Dragoon, camping in the tumbled rocks surrounding the town that night. The next morning they moved out just at daylight and rode down the main street of Dragoon past its mean scatter of adobes without stopping. Half a dozen loungers, taking the early morning sun from porches and verandas, watched them pass without comment or salute. To the east of the town Vent led the way down a narrow draw and past a small house, where a man in bib overalls sat on the front porch and drank coffee. Beside his elbow lay a Winchester rifle and a shell belt bearing a .44 Smith and Wesson breaktop six shot hung around his lean hips.

As they rounded in at the gate, the man nodded and invited them to step down and rest their saddles.

"Thanks, friend, but we're bound to make Tombstone tonight," Vent said.

The man nodded, observing drily, "A lot of men hurried to that town. Some of them ain't never gonna leave it."

Vent grinned. Chan nodded, touched his black gambler's hat and rode on just as a woman with a tired, lined face came to the door. Voices carried clear in that rarefied desert air and Vent heard her ask, "Who were them fellers, paw?"

"Just some grubline riders," he replied. "Said they was going to Tombstone. Like as not they'll add to the boot hill population . . ."

And the voice faded away and Vent glanced at Chan and said, "Like as not . . ."

Hard riding put them in Charleston by ten o'clock. They had found it without trouble, having followed the light glow from a dozen buildings, including a large saloon. Sitting his horse in the middle of the main street, Vent had his look and remembered the night he and the Preacher and Owney Sharp went to war here with the hangman of the Bandera and his men. Victorio had helped him in that fight and now he wondered if these people would remember and find a reason to call up trouble for that night's work.

"I had a set-to here once," Vent said.

"I heard," Chan nodded.

"You thirsty?"

"We got a choice; a river full of water or a coupla shots of old gut ripper," Chan countered.

Vent thought about it some more then tapped his saddlebags and said, "I just happen to have a bit of snake bite medicine here. Let's move on to the river and fill the canteens and see if we can't make the Nogales road tonight."

"Hell, it's only about ten miles from here," Chan said and gigged up his big black and Vent spoke softly to the Appaloosa and they rode through the town and found a cut leading to the river and pulled in to let the horses drink. As they sat waiting for them to finish, several riders rode out of the brush on the opposite bank and splashed into the water. Vent could see them plainly in the moonlight, but knew he and Chan were hidden in the deep shadows cast by overhanging trees and the bank behind them.

Not wanting to get shot by a nervous cowboy, Vent

called out, "Nice night, boys," and the riders pulled up their horses in the middle of the river, then one sang out, "Who's that?"

"Just a couple of travelers," Vent answered and watched them come on. When they reached the east bank, the man who had answered them rode over and had his look and said softly, "Ain't you the gent they call Leatherhand?"

Vent smiled in the darkness and his teeth flashed briefly in the moonlight as he said, "I'm Vent Torrey."

"Nice night for a ride, Mr. Torrey," the rider said and turned his horse and rode to where his friends waited and spoke briefly to them, then led the way out of the cut.

Vent gave them ten minutes to clear the bluff and then rode boldly into the river with Chan close behind. Once on the opposite bank, they put their horses to a sharp trot and followed a rough trail leading due west. Fifty yards out Vent pulled up, took the canteens and returned on foot to refill them. That night they camped half a mile from the Huachuca road.

Three days later they were riding into the small village of Covered Wells and Vent, whose side still gave him problems, decided to stay in the quiet town for a couple of days and rest up.

Chan grinned and observed, "I'm ready. I got saddle galls on saddle galls."

They found a water trough in front of a livery stable and allowed the animals to drink, then turned into the cool interior and dismounted.

"Howdy, boys," a broad-shouldered man wearing a leather apron and carrying a pair of hoof nippers, greeted them. "What can I do for you?"

"Want to stall these animals for two days," Vent told him. "Plenty of good grain, good hay and a rubdown. The Appy has a loose shoe so reckon it's time to tack on a new set."

Chan led his black forward and kneeling, pointed to a crack in one hoof and said, "Can you do something to stop that from getting worse?"

The liveryman stared at Chan for a long moment, probably wondering what the hell he is, Vent figured, then he lifted the hoof and examined it and said, "I can fix it, but you probably should give this old pony a rest first chance you get."

"They a place rents rooms in this town?" Vent asked.

Dropping the hoof, the liveryman walked to the door and pointed to a long, low building half a block down the dusty single street bisecting the village and said, "The widow Jenkins rents rooms, but she's a teetotaler. Won't stand for no drinkin' and gets madder airy a wet hen iffin a feller brings in one of them local *señoritas* for a little playtime."

"Sounds like a right upstanding lady any man would be proud to call mother," Vent observed.

"She's that, all right," the liveryman agreed. Nodding at the horses, he said, "Shoeing will cost you two dollars. Fixing that black's hoof will be another dollar and the feed and care of the two of them is another three dollars . . . that's six dollars . . ."

Chan dug out a ten dollar gold piece and handed it to the man and said, "The extra is for extra good care of these horses. They still got a long way to go," and he turned and followed Vent downstreet to a small cantina.

The place was filled with shadows and coolness. The bartender, an elderly Mexican, looked up from reading a Spanish language newspaper and smiled widely. "*Señors*, what will you have today?" There was no one else in the place.

They ordered whiskey and when it came, Vent tasted it, made a wiry face and asked, "Who makes this stuff for you?"

The Mexican grinned and said, "Fellow named Charlie

201

Catch-A-Fly; Indio. Lives out on the Lukeville road. Pretty good, huh?''

Chan shook his head and setting the glass down, asked, ''You got any tequila?''

Smiling broadly the man turned and lifted a bottle from a shelf behind the bar and set out two new glasses. Pouring them full, he went to a small cooler and brought them several slices of lemon in a saucer and produced a salt cellar, then beaming, said, ''One dollar, please.''

Vent paid with a cartwheel and they took the bottle and found chairs against the wall. Looking at the Mexican, who had returned to his paper, Vent called, ''Got anything to eat?''

Nodding, the proprietor went into the back room and returned with a tray. Two steaming bowls of chili and a stack of soft flour tortillas crowded it as he came across the room. The food was good and they ate two bowls apiece and drank several shots of the fiery tequila then rose, paid the owner, who charged them a dollar for the meal, and went out.

Noted Chan, ''Things a bit slow around here. The date on that paper was eight months old.''

They stayed at Mrs. Jenkins's hotel for two nights and left early the morning of the third day, their food and water replenished and the horses reshod and rested.

The trail south was wide enough to accommodate a wagon, but Vent noted it had been so long since one traveled this way that any tracks left by such a vehicle had long since been blown over by sand. It was a hard, harsh land they rode through and the heat was a 110-degree battering ram that pushed them down in the saddle and drained away the urge to talk.

So, they rode in silence until the heat became unbearable, then they sought the shade of a small grove of stunted trees, and, watering the horses from their hats, removed saddles and allowed them to roll in the dust of a nearby dry streambed, then each man rubbed down his mount with handfuls of dry grass and fitted them with nosebags of grain. While the horses ground up the feed between their teeth, Vent matched a coin with Chan to see who took first watch and won. Stretching out on his saddle blanket, he was almost immediately asleep.

They spent the heat of the afternoon sleeping in turns and when the sun dropped below the horizon, taking the high temperatures with it, they saddled up, allowed the horses another hatful of water and rode south.

The rising sun found them sitting just off the trail five miles from Puerto Peñasco.

"I think we best lay out here until after dark, then have a look at this place," Vent suggested.

Chan nodded. "Chances are, our friends have some contacts here or they wouldn't have come here in the first place. . . . Even if they didn't know anybody, the Magician's been here long enough to have made some friends. He could have a neat little warning network set up among the villagers."

So they waited until full dark, then rode to the outskirts of town, where they split up, Chan riding toward the gulf and Vent circling to the east. When he could no longer see the tall shape of the half-breed, Vent gigged his horse lightly and rode around the outskirts of the village. As he progressed from one mean shack to another, dogs suddenly rushed from beneath steps to snap viciously at his horse's hooves, only to receive a resounding kick in the ribs that sent them yelping back to cover. Doors were flung open and men peered forth, challenging, *"Quién es?"*

Vent continued on without answering, then he was at the south edge of the village and decided to ride on in as if he belonged there. Clucking to the big Appaloosa, he cake-walked him along the single main street, keeping a sharp eye on doors and windows. The smell of the sea came clearly to him and he could hear the sigh of waves as they rushed up the beach and foamed away as they backed off for another run.

The lights of the cantina were dim against the dirty cloth stretched over the window openings, but a single beam splashed through the front door and into the street, bringing with it the sound of an out-of-tune piano and the dulcet tones of a woman singing a Spanish ballad he couldn't quite place. Cutting down an alley, he came up behind the cantina and stepping from his horse, tied the reins to a pole corral and quietly walked to the back door.

Standing clear of the light he looked the interior over and when he didn't see his man, moved to the other side of the door and examined the dim recesses of the room and saw the Magician sitting at a table in the gunfighter's chair, his back against the wall, a bottle before him and a deck of cards in his hands.

The opposite side of the room contained the bar and Vent counted five men leaning there drinking. One was obviously a *vaquero* from a nearby ranch, two of them had the stink of fish on them and probably worked on a boat, the third man was white and wore two guns, a Bowie knife, dirty clothes and needed a shave. He had his arm around a saloon girl and was nuzzling her neck. The fourth man was dressed in the white favored by peons and was probably a farmer. A man played a piano and a girl with a young-old face sang softly.

The man behind the bar was an obese monster and looking at him Vent figured if someone rendered him out for his fat, they'd get enough to last a year. He waddled back and forth behind the plank, a Mexican cheroot between his teeth, a glass of tequila in his hand. A glass on the bar top held a pistol, barrel downward, butt within easy grasping range.

Vent stepped through the door and placed his back to the bar. When the owner started his way with an expectant look on his face, Vent raised a hand, palm outward, and the man stopped, then looked at the Magician and the white man, obviously trying to determine which one of them this tall gringo was after. The piano went dead and the girl suddenly broke off her song in mid-stanza.

Then the Magician raised his eyes and looked at Vent and said, "You've come a long way to die, Leatherhand."

When the bartender started to edge down to where the pistol stood up from the glass invitingly, Vent said without looking at him, "You touch that glass, *amigo*, and I'm going to blow it all over you."

The bartender stopped and placed both hands on the bar, suddenly deciding to remain neutral.

The white man leaning on the bar stepped clear of the girl and asked softly, "Who the hell are you?"

Vent did not look at him, but merely replied, "The man who's going to kill you if you don't go over to that table in the corner and sit down. While you're there, put those guns on the floor."

The man looked at Vent and said in amazement, "You're *loco*."

"Better do what he says, Mr. Smith," the Magician warned. "This here gent's handle is Leatherhand. He's lost count of the men he's put down."

"Hell, it ain't my put in anyway," the man called Smith declared and he walked to the table, carefully removed his guns and placed them on the floor and sat down well away from them.

"Good judgment," Vent said.

"You know you can't beat me," the Magician said.

"That fast, huh?"

The gambler smiled and placed the cards in front of him, carefully squared the edges, then let his hands lay on each side of them. "Nobody's ever beaten me, or even come close . . ."

Vent smiled, but there was no mirth in it. "I guess that makes us a club," he intoned, watching the Magician's eyes.

Then, from the corner of his eye Vent saw movement at the back door and flicked his eyes that way as Hitch Hawks raised his gun to fire. Vent's eyes flashed back to the table and saw the gun appear in the Magician's hand and he knew he couldn't beat him as he fell away and let the *shuriken* drop from his sleeve and sent it screaming across the room to bury itself in the gambler's throat. Then Hawks's gun thundered.

But Vent was already falling and the slug snapped past his head to bury itself in the adobe wall as he drew like bouncing flame, and twisting toward the back door, fired at the fleeting shadow that was Hawks dodging away and knew he had missed him clean.

Wheeling back toward the Magician from his position on the floor, Vent centered the bore of the .44 on the gambler's head and waited.

He still held the gun, but now it began to sag in his hand as he made choking, gurgling noises around the five-pointed star buried in his jugular.

The gun fell to the table from fingers no longer able to hold it and the Magician croaked, "Lady . . . Luck . . .," and blood gushed from his mouth onto the fallen gun and he fell forward and died. As the patrons stared, the Magician's body slowly slid sideways from its chair and dropped to the floor, looking like a well-dressed scarecrow that someone had hurled red paint on.

Vent rose and walked toward the body, still keeping an eye on the bartender, when a sudden hammering roar of fast-triggered guns came to him from somewhere down by the bay and he whirled and ran out the back door and swung aboard the Appaloosa and leaped him away down a narrow alley.

He was running full out when he hit the beach and then he heard two more shots from north of the village and saw the streaks of fire from hot barrels and rode toward them, punching the single exploded round from his .44 and replacing it with a fresh load.

A hundred yards from where the fight was in progress, the Appy suddenly hesitated, then leaped high, almost unseating Vent as he cleared a fishing boat that had been left face down on the beach. The horse landed hard, almost fell, then caught his balance and whirled on and then Vent saw Chan ride from a stand of trees and lift his gun and fire three times. From somewhere out in the night two slamming shots answered him, followed by the thunder of hard-run horses fading toward the upper end of the gulf. When Chan would have pursued them, Vent called, "Arkie, wait," and watched the half-breed turn his black and come trotting back.

Pulling in, he punched out his empties and grinned at Vent in the moonlight and observed, "I heard two shots. The Magician?"

"He's dead, but it wasn't the bullet that killed him. I used a *shuriken*," Vent said.

"Well, I'll be damned," Chan marveled, then asked, "What were the shots? His?"

Vent shook his head. "No, one was mine. The other Hawks's. He laid for me at the back door. Bastards had me whipsawed. I nailed the Magician with the star and got a shot off at Hawks. Sorta discouraged him . . . You get lead in him or that Papago?"

"No, but they damned near did for me," Chan said ruefully. "I forgot about that Indian. Saw Hawks riding like hell along the beach and went after him. The Papago was hiding behind a fishing boat. Popped up and cut down on me. Damned if I can figure how the hell he missed me.''

Vent grinned. ''Luck of the draw. Let's go back to the cantina and do some cleanup work.''

When they returned to the cantina, they found the local police there. A young lieutenant wearing a neatly clipped mustache was bent over the Magician's body and when Vent and Chan came in the back door, he rose and came down the bar and leaning there, said mildly, ''Would you gentlemen mind explaining what happened here.'' His English was letter perfect.

Vent looked around, noted the two officers in their brown uniforms leaning against the wall near the door, rifles held casually in their hands, and nodded. ''Been looking for this feller for two months. Kidnapper of women, murderer and wanted in my country by the United States Army authorities.''

''Do you represent your country here?'' the lieutenant asked.

''I have been commissioned by General Crook at Fort Bowie to deliver this man to him so that he may be charged. He placed no restrictions on how far or where I might go to effect his return.''

''I would like to see that commission,'' the officer stated.

Vent removed a folded sheet of legal-appearing paper from his chap pocket and handed it to the officer, who scanned it and handed it back. ''It seems you are telling the truth, Mr. Torrey.''

Vent said, ''Thank you,'' and walked to the Magician's body and bent and removed the *shuriken*. As he pulled it free, a gout of blood poured from the wound and the man named Smith said, ''God,'' and Vent looked up at him and said nothing as he wiped the star off on the dead man's shirt.

The lieutenant came over then and looking at the star, said, "That's an odd thing for a man to use in a duel. What is it?"

Handing it to him Vent said, "It's called a *shuriken* and my friend here taught me its use."

Handing it back, the officer shook his head and asked, "Why didn't you just shoot him?"

"He was a magician. He made guns appear and disappear. No one could outdraw him. I did not want to die just yet."

The lieutenant nodded his understanding of that and then glancing toward the back door, asked, "Who were you chasing on the beach?"

Vent walked to the bar and pointing to a bottle of tequila said, "A man named Hawks. He sold guns to the Apaches in my country."

"Ah, we know of this man Hawks," the officer said and held up a finger to the bartender, who dug out a third glass and poured drinks for Vent, Chan and the lieutenant.

"You have heard of Hawks?" Vent asked.

Scowling, the officer said quietly, "He killed a friend of mine in Fronteras; a policeman. He and that Indian. The Rurales pursued him in this direction but lost him in the mountains. He is a very dangerous man."

Vent tossed off his drink and said coldly, "In ten days he will be no more," and nodding toward the body, asked, "Will you have need of us?"

The officer shook his head. "I am Lieutenant Delgado. I wish you Godspeed . . . *Bueno caza* . . ."

Vent smiled and said, "Gracias," and led Chan out the back door to the horses.

They followed the coastline until midnight. Hawks and his Indian's tracks showed plainly in the light of a half moon. They were up again at dawn and once more fell to tracking the fugitives. Two days put them in the fishing village of Golfo de Santa Clara, where they replenished their supplies, took on three extra canteens of water and after resting away the afternoon, took the wagon road north toward San Luis Rio Colorado. Vent had stared down at the double set of tracks until he knew he could follow them through the coal heaps of hell and when they headed north, they were there, plain to see.

Nodding at the tracks, Vent said, "Looks like those boys' horses are beginning to feel the ride."

Looking down at their own mouths, Chan observed drily, "Have you taken a look at these old ponies lately?"

They rode into San Luis on the banks of the Colorado River at eight o'clock and searched out a livery stable, where they left the tired horses and found a restaurant. Sitting with their backs to the wall, they ordered steak, eggs and a huge bowl of fried potatoes, topped it off with a gallon of coffee and ate in silence, oblivious to the stares of the other patrons, who had taken their inventory when they walked through the door.

Sighing, Vent pushed back his plate, dug out tobacco and rolled a cigarette, fired it up and refilled his coffee cup as a man wearing townsmen's clothes and a flat-crowned hat walked in, looked around, and seeing them, came across the room.

Stopping before their table, the man pulled back his coattails, hooked his thumbs in a shell belt holding twin Russian .44s and said mildly, "I'm the marshal here."

Vent looked at him and asked, "What's an American doing policing a town in Mexico?"

The man smiled. "Name's Carlos Ramos, born in Mexico to a Mexican father and an American mother."

Vent glanced at Chan and said, "Name's Vent Torrey from Missouri and this here feller's called Arkie Chan," and watched the marshal's eyes flatten out as a look of caution washed across his face. Removing his thumbs from his gunbelt, he let his hands fall and said, "Heard of you boys. Kinda off your usual trails, ain't you?"

"Looking for a man," Vent said. "Feller sold a load of repeaters to the Apaches over in Arizona Territory. Got a lotta folks put under."

Nodding at a chair Ramos asked, "Mind if I sit," and when Vent inclined his head, slid into it and leaning his elbows on the table, asked, "Anything I can do?"

Vent shook his head. "Don't think so, marshal. Feller may be here, but I figure he rested a day or two and moved on. We've been about two days behind him."

"You working for the law, Mr. Torrey?" the marshal asked.

"The Army," Vent said.

"Mind telling me who you're looking for?"

"Man named Hitch Hawks . . ."

"Was he sided by an Indian, a Papago?"

Vent glanced at Chan and said, "He was. You see him?"

"He stayed at the hotel down the street one night. The Indian slept in the livery with their horses. Feller was plenty rank. Old-timer; seen a lot of hard miles . . ."

"Did he have some fingers missing on his right hand?" Vent asked.

Ramos nodded. "Yes. Looked like they'd been blowed off."

"They were," Vent replied, but didn't elaborate.

The waitress came to the table and smiling at the marshal, asked, "You want some coffee, El Jefe?"

Ramos nodded and after she went away, he said, "I saw your man ride west. He crossed the river at dawn this morning. Headed toward the El Camino del Diablo."

Vent stared at him. "Hell, no man in his right mind would cross that place, not now, he wouldn't."

Ramos nodded in agreement. "There's water out there

if you know where it is. That's probably why Hawks has the Papago with him. He'd know.''

"Have you ever crossed there, Marshal?" Chan asked.

"Once, and it was hell. They's graves from the Colorado to Quitobaquito and at the springs at Tinajas Altas, I looked at a hill where forty men have been buried. It's called the Mesita de los Muertos . . .''

"The place of death," Vent spoke softly.

"They all died of thirst within 200 feet of water," the marshal said.

"It would be a thing Hawks would attempt," Vent said and rose and dropping a handful of coins on the table, added, "We will leave here in the morning."

The marshal nodded, then turning his head as they started past him, said, "If I can be of assistance . . . ?"

"We'll let you know, marshal," Vent replied, then asked, "tell me, why did you come to us in the first place?"

He smiled. "When two dangerous-looking *pistoleros* enter my jurisdiction, I always check them out."

"Get shot at often?" Chan asked mildly.

"Quite often," Ramos acknowledged with a grin.

"Adios," Vent said and led the way to the sidewalk.

The two men sat beneath the shade of an overhanging boulder and stared down at the trail below them. It led into the caldron of El Camino del Diablo. As far west as the eye could see, the dry, sun-tortured land stretched away, a place fit only for centipedes, lizards and snakes. It was hot; removing his bandana from around his neck, Vent used it to wipe away the sweat that had accumulated on his face, then reknotted it. Pushing his hat lower on his forehead to shield his eyes from the shimmering waves reflected off the barren ground, he slouched lower against the rock and let his eyelids half close.

Chan had removed his coat, as Vent had shed his heavy

chaps, and now the gambler sat in his shirt-sleeves and fondled a deck of cards as he lay out a solitare hand on his saddle blanket. Their horses were tied in the shade fifty feet back in the rocks, where they stood with heads lowered against the heat and patiently awaited their masters' next move.

Two days' hard riding had put them ahead of Hawks and his Papago and Vent knew that if the old man really planned to cross the El Camino del Diablo, he would pass this way. When he did Vent would kill him.

When their quarry failed to appear after six hours of patient waiting, Vent said, "Reckon he rode back into Mexico or followed the Colorado north?"

"No," Chan guessed. "I think he and his Injun probably went to ground in this heat and plan to travel after the sun goes down. They'll be along."

As it turned out Chan was right. The last rays of the sun were turning the desert to crimson when Hawks and the Indian suddenly appeared 300 yards out on the desert. Vent spotted them first and cursing, ran to his saddle and jerked his rifle free.

"What the hell happened?" Chan called, and Vent turned and ran to a low rock, dropped on his stomach and leveled the rifle over the makeshift rest.

"They cut away from the trail," he said, and centering the sights on Hawks's back, squeezed the trigger.

The big 38.40 rifle slammed its echo out across the desert and Vent watched the round kick up dust fifty feet behind the two men, who suddenly put spurs to their horses and jumped them into a run. Cursing wildly, Vent leveled the rifle again and fired. The Papago had been riding to Hawks's left, but then cut across behind him just as Vent fired and caught the heavy slug, dropping immediately to the ground in a tumbling, loose-jointed roll that fetched him up against a cactus motionless.

"Damn!" Chan exclaimed. "That must be 400 yards," and then Hawks was whirling back and Vent fired again and missed and watched the old man spin his horse to a stop, look down at the Papago and apparently finding him dead, gallop away west. Vent fired once more but the range defied the 38.40 and he wished fervently for a Sharps.

"He's gone," Vent said as he rose and fed shells back into the rifle.

Chan stood up and gazed out into the inferno of El Camino del Diablo and shook his head and observed, "In more ways than one, my friend. Without the Papago, he'll never find the springs. He's a dead man riding."

Vent was inclined to agree with him, but decided to make certain. "We'll remain here three days and if he doesn't ride back out of there in that time, we'll know he's buzzard bait."

Chan looked at him and asked, "What if he makes it across?"

"Then he will have earned the right to live a little longer," Vent replied bleakly.

They waited three days and when Hawks failed to show, Vent reluctantly saddled the Appaloosa and he and Chan rode from that blistering hell.

Epilogue

Harp Denton and his lady were married at the Monger Ranch in one of the largest weddings ever held in the San Pedro Valley. He went to his fate with a grin on his face and when he saw Vent Torrey and Arkie Chan in the crowd watching the knot being tied, he winked and everybody thought he had something in his eye.

Rebecca and Wolf set up housekeeping on Wolf's ranch near Tucson and a month after the death of her father a lawyer rode into the yard, smiled at the couple sitting on the veranda and informed Mrs. Wolf her inheritance was intact, that her father had never touched it. Overly, a desperate man, had used the ploy to win her and Wolf to his side.

To the lawyer's amazement, the lady broke into tears.

Vent and Chan visited Fort Bowie and while taking their ease on the veranda of Colonel Bedlam's quarters, were approached by Nantaje, who squatted in the dust and looking up at them, said solemnly, "You kill sumbitch magic man. Better hunter than Nantaje. He only catch bullet."

One afternoon Chan saddled his big black and stepping aboard, rode across the parade ground and stopping at Bedlam's quarters, looked down at Vent, who sat in an old

215

rocker with his hat over his eyes, and observed, "This here feller's about done for, horse. Me, I can't stand to see a good man fade away like this . . . Let's go back to Bodie," and he rode to the gate, stopped and without looking back, waved a hand and was gone.

Two days later, Vent saddled the Appaloosa, shoved his rifle in the scabbard, fastened two days grub behind the cantleboard, and rode to where Bedlam and Speers were sitting in chairs under a large oak tree, sipping iced tea. Looking down at them, he said, "Gentlemen, reckon I'll go look at the other side of the mountain."

Bedlam smiled, and lifting his drink, saluted Vent: "To the swiftest goes the race; good running," and he drank the glass dry.

"Where are you heading?" Speers asked, and Vent smiled and replied, "Tucson. I kinda like that town," and rode from the fort.

Watching him go, Speers turned to Bedlam and asked, "Why Tucson?"

Bedlam looked wise. "A lady," he said.

"Now that makes sense," Speers observed.

Watch for

THE LAST RIDE

next in the LEATHERHAND series
from Pinnacle Books

coming in May!